Harwinton Got His Middle Name

Enjoy!
Linda Machado
2004

Linda Machado

XULON PRESS

Library of Congress Control Number: 2002110753
ISBN 1-591601-47-9

Xulon Press
11350 Random Hills Road
Suite 800
Fairfax, VA 22030
(703) 279-6511
XulonPress.com

To order additional copies,
call 1-866-909-BOOK (2665).

A Note from the Author

Welcome to the first story in the Harwinton Christian Bear series!

This book has been written to bring the salvation message of Jesus Christ to children of all ages—both deaf and hearing. The language of the Deaf is American Sign Language (ASL). ASL is a beautiful language in its own right with its own grammatical structure—a structure that is difficult to capture on paper. Therefore, for the ease of young readers, the dialogue for the deaf characters, Ranger George and Betty Goodwill, has been written in straight English sentences.

Also, for those readers who are unfamiliar with the teletypewriter (TTY) used by the Deaf, a brief note of explanation is provided here for Chapter 14.

TTYs are used by the Deaf to communicate by telephone. Some models are equipped with a printer for which a special roll of paper is needed. If the printer is turned on during a TTY call, it will print out the conversation. The lower case (small) letters are words typed by you and the upper case (capital) letters are words typed by the other person. To save time, punctuation, such as commas and periods, is not always used.

The use of GA means Go Ahead. GA tells the other person it's his or her turn to type. The letter Q, when typed at the end of a sentence denotes a question. The use of SK or SKSK means Stop Keying. It signifies the end of the conversation.

Hope you enjoy the story! SKSK

Contents

CHAPTER 1

The Dark Forest, a Tree and a Bumblebee

The Dark Forest. To the people who lived in The Lost City, it was a wildlife park, a place to have fun and see the animals. But to little Harwinton Bear, it was home.

Deep inside the forest, beyond the field where the honeysuckle grew, stood a huge cluster of thick bushes and tall trees. Snugly hidden from view, behind those trees, was the roomy den where the Bear family lived. There were seven in Harwinton's family: Poppa, Momma, his big brother, Wallum, and his three older sisters, Emma-Sue, Mary-Barbara and Trina.

Harwinton's best friend was a young cottontail named Benjamin Uriah Maaziah Pekahiah Elisha Rabbit.

"What kind of a name is that?" asked Harwinton, when they first met.

"Some relative's," sighed the rabbit. "I don't like it. It's dumb."

"I've got an idea," said Harwinton. "Let's take the first letter of all your names and see what we get. B-U-M-P-E-R. Bumper. How 'bout if I call you that?"

"Sounds good to me," agreed the rabbit happily.

Harwinton and Bumper spent many hours together roaming through the forest, peeking behind trees and under rocks to see what they could find. One day, after returning from an uneventful expedition, they plopped down under a maple tree in Harwinton's backyard.

"What shall we do now?" asked Bumper as he aimlessly tossed some pebbles.

"I'm thinking," replied the bear.

Harwinton's gaze fell upon a familiar sight—the huge fir tree that towered above the Bear family's den. His eyes widening with the excitement of a great idea, the little cub began to run toward the tree.

"C'mon, Bumper," he called.

"What are we going to do?"

"Not 'we', me," answered Harwinton. "I'm going

to climb this tree."

"But your parents told you to stay away from it until you could climb better!" exclaimed Bumper.

"I *can* climb better," insisted the bear. "You saw me go up that elm tree today."

"Yeah, but it wasn't as high."

"I'm older now and I can do it. You be the lookout in case one of my sisters sees us and tattletales."

"I hope you know what you're doing," answered Bumper nervously as his friend began to inch his way up the giant tree.

Harwinton had already climbed more than halfway when Emma-Sue came outside to gather some berries for supper. Out of the corner of her eye she saw something moving.

She looked and looked again. "MOMMA! MOMMA!" she cried. "Come quick! Harwinton's up in the giant tree!"

Momma Bear hurried to the backyard. "HARWINTON BEAR!" she shouted. "Get down from there this instant."

"Coming, Momma!" he answered. But *how* do I get down? wondered the now very frightened cub. Slowly, he started moving backward. How high up he was! How small everything seemed on the ground below. Feeling a little dizzy, he closed his eyes for a brief moment. Suddenly, Harwinton started to slip.

Horrified, Bumper watched as his friend fell

away from the tree, did a somersault in the air and crash-landed into the honey barrel that Wallum Bear had just finished filling.

The barrel broke and honey spilled out everywhere. Bumper stayed long enough to make sure Harwinton wasn't hurt and then raced for home as fast as his legs could carry him.

"*What* did we tell you?" scolded Momma severely. "Didn't you listen?"

"What's the trouble, Momma?" called out Poppa Bear, who was just coming home.

"Our son tried to climb the big tree," she explained. "He fell and this is what happened."

The sight of the honey-covered little bear sitting in the middle of the broken barrel was too much for Poppa. In spite of himself, he began to shake with his deep, jolly laugh.

"It's *not* funny!" cried Momma Bear. "He could have been hurt. And what about the honey?"

"We can get more, Momma. Are you all right, son?" asked Poppa Bear, as he helped Harwinton to his feet.

"Yes."

"Now do you understand why we told you not to climb the tree?"

The cub nodded. "I won't do it again, I promise."

"Harwinton," continued Poppa Bear quietly, but firmly, "for your punishment, you will clean up the mess you made. And when Wallum goes for honey, you will go with him until all of it is replaced."

"Yes, sir," answered Harwinton meekly.

"Come on," sighed Momma. "We'll have to clean you up before you can clean the mess."

Harwinton solemnly stood by while Momma, without saying a word, filled the washtub with hot, sudsy water. The small bear dutifully climbed in and scrubbed off the sticky, amber-colored liquid.

"I'm really sorry, Momma," said Harwinton as she dried his ears with a soft towel.

"I know you are," she replied.

"Are you still angry?"

Momma stopped and looked into Harwinton's sad, but hopeful, face. "No," she answered.

Harwinton smiled and gave her a big hug. "I love you, Momma," he whispered.

"I love you, too."

The next few mornings, Harwinton trailed after Wallum to help him search for honey. It seemed they would never finish filling the new, bigger barrel Poppa Bear had made.

"Now don't break this one," warned Wallum after Harwinton had poured in the last golden drop. Then, stooping down, Wallum added, "When you get a little bit older, I'll show you how to climb the big tree, okay?"

Harwinton beamed at his brother and nodded

eagerly.

Momma Bear came out to inspect the barrel. "You've both done a fine job," she said.

"Momma, may I go play with Bumper today? Please?"

"Yes, Harwinton, you may go," she answered. "But try to stay out of trouble."

"Thank you, Momma. I will," he said. The cub scampered along the familiar path to the edge of the honeysuckle field and the burrow where the Rabbit family lived.

"Bumper!" he called.

After a few minutes, a small head peeked around the door of the burrow. "Oh! Hi, Harwinton," said Bumper in a sad voice.

"Wanna come with me to the field?" asked the bear.

"I can't."

"Why?"

"I uh..."

"Who is it, Bumper?" called a pleasant voice from inside the burrow. The door opened wider. "Why, Harwinton! How nice to see you."

"Good Morning, Mrs. Rabbit," said the bear cheerfully. "May Bumper come outside and play?"

"I'm sorry," she answered, "but he has a slight earache, and I want to keep him home for a day or two."

"Hope you feel better soon, Bump," said Harwinton.

"So do I," sniffed Bumper, his long ears drooping even longer.

"You'd better come in now, dear," said Mrs. Rabbit. "It's time for your nap. Thank you for stopping by, Harwinton. Say 'hello' to your family for us."

"I will. Thank you, Mrs. Rabbit," called Harwinton, as he turned to go. "See you later, Bumper."

"Bye," replied Bumper, slowly waving his paw. He watched until his friend disappeared over the hill. The little rabbit heaved a big sigh and closed the door. How he wished he could go, too.

And no wonder! It was one of those just-right summer days with lots of sunshine and puffy white clouds that made funny shapes in the sky. A perfect day for an adventure, thought Harwinton as he rolled around in the soft, green grass. A gentle breeze brought the smell of a favorite fragrance—honeysuckle! The bear decided to take a closer look at the beautiful blossoms. Sitting on the ground, he carefully bent one of the flowers towards his small nose and took a big whiff.

"OUCH!" he shouted.

"And just what do you think *you're* doing?" demanded an angry, teeny-tiny voice.

Harwinton stared, wide-eyed. There, in the center of the flower, his teeny-tiny hands on his teeny-tiny hips, stood a mad-as-a-hornet bumblebee.

"I just wanted to smell it," explained the cub.

"Well, go find another one," the bee replied crossly. "This is *my* flower."

Rubbing his sore nose, Harwinton ran away. When he got home, he tried to hide the swelling, but Momma knew something was wrong.

"Come here," she called softly. "What happened this time?"

Climbing onto her lap, Harwinton tearfully told her about the field, the flower and the angry bee. "Did I do a bad thing, Momma?"

"Of course not," she answered as she lightly rubbed salve on his nose and bandaged it. "Those flowers belong to everybody. Besides, you didn't know he was there. But why did you run away? You shouldn't have let him intimidate you."

"What's 'timdate mean, Momma?"

"In-tim-i-date," repeated Momma slowly so he could learn the word. "It means to be afraid of something or somebody."

"Did you ever get afraid and run away?"

"Yes, Harwinton," she answered, kissing him gently on the nose, "but as I grew up there were times when even though I was really afraid, I needed to be strong and brave."

"Will I have those times, too?"

"I wish I could say that you won't; but when you do I hope you'll remember what I've told you."

"I will, Momma."

CHAPTER 2

FIRE!

Days passed and the cold winds of winter came upon The Dark Forest. Harwinton stayed in the den with his family and did not see his friend Bumper until spring. Both had grown a little and while they still liked to go on adventures together, they had more responsibilities at home. Bumper, who was the oldest of the boys in his family, now had a baby sister named Bunni.

One warm, summer morning, Harwinton stopped by. "Hey, Bumper," he called. "Let's go exploring."

"Hi, Harwinton! Sorry, but I can't right now. My parents are going somewhere with my brothers and need me to watch Bunni. Maybe after lunch."

"Okay, I'll come back later. Bye!" Wondering what to do, Harwinton ambled off in the direction of the campgrounds. Poppa Bear had often sternly warned him to stay away from them, especially at this time of year when people from The Lost City were allowed to visit the forest. But Harwinton's curiosity won out, and he went anyway.

Safely hidden among some thick bushes, the young bear watched as the humans played, fished and ate. He didn't like it when he saw they had built fires to cook the fish they had caught. He knew fire could be very dangerous and sighed with relief when the last of the flames went out. After the humans had left, Harwinton ventured from his hiding place to search for leftovers from the picnic lunches.

As he hungrily licked at the last of a peanut butter and jelly sandwich, the familiar smell of burning wood drifted by. At first, he paid no attention to it—until the increasing wind caused the smell to become stronger. A heavy fog began to fill the campgrounds, darkening the bright summer day. That's funny, thought the bear, the sun was just shining a minute ago.

The alarmed cries from a flock of birds made him look up. Rising skyward, and spreading swiftly, was an enormous black cloud—A FOREST FIRE! Just beyond the entrance to the campgrounds, Harwinton saw angry, red-orange flames shooting out from the trees and melting away into the ugly darkness. Terrified, the young bear started for home.

Back at the Bear family's den, the fire raged closer and closer. While Poppa helped the older ones, Momma frantically searched for her youngest cub.

"Poppa, I can't find Harwinton," she cried. "He must be out in the forest somewhere!"

"We have no choice, Momma," answered Poppa. "We have to leave *now*!"

He pushed her ahead of him towards the one path that was still open, while above them the trees started to blaze.

"RUN!" bellowed Poppa Bear.

CRASH! A large, burning limb fell, blocking Harwinton's way. Jumping back, he turned and ran down a narrow, side path that led to a stream. As he reached the end of the path, a deafening roar made him stop. A few feet away from him, a herd of frightened animals was stampeding down the clearing beside the stream. Horrified, the bear watched as friends pushed each other aside to be first to cross to safety. Suddenly, a breathless figure darted past Harwinton, heading for the clearing.

"Stop!" called the bear.

Startled by the voice, the figure dove under a small cluster of berry bushes. Hiding in the shadows, it crouched down beneath the low branches and waited.

Somewhere on a trail near the burrow, the Rabbit family struggled to see and breathe in the fire's thick smoke. As they held tightly to one another's paws for support, Bunni realized her oldest brother was missing.

"Momma!" she shrieked. "Where's Bumper?"

"I thought he was behind you!" exclaimed Mrs. Rabbit, turning to look back.

"Keep moving!" ordered Poppa Rabbit. "There's no time to lose!"

Keeping his eye on the spot where the figure lay, Harwinton cautiously approached the berry bushes. In the smoky light, he could see the shape of its long ears.

"Bumper? Is that you?"

"Oh, Harwinton! Yes, it is!" He scurried over to his friend. "It's just awful," continued the rabbit in a trembling voice. "My family and I were running away when I went back to the burrow to make sure everyone was out. But there was so much smoke, I lost sight of them, and now I don't know where they are!"

"Do you know where the fire started?"

"Somewhere near the honeysuckle field. The rangers are trying to fight the fire, but it's spreading too fast."

"The honeysuckle field," cried Harwinton with alarm. "That's not far from our den. I have to go back!"

Bumper put out a paw to stop him. "You *can't* go that way now. It's too dangerous. And your family would want you safe."

Harwinton sat down on the hard ground. Tears began to roll down his cheeks and splash onto his paws. "Don't be afraid," said Bumper, trying not to cry as well. "I'm alone, too. We'll stick together. But we'd better get out of here while there's still time."

The word 'afraid' reminded Harwinton of Momma's lesson to not let anything intimidate him. He realized this was a time he needed to be strong and brave.

Moving quickly, the two friends crossed the clearing and the stream. When they reached the top of the hill on the other side, Harwinton looked back. In the distance he saw a tall tree toppling over. He wondered if it was the same one he had fallen out of the day he had broken the honey barrel.

"Harwinton!" shouted Bumper impatiently.

"Coming!" answered the bear. "Where are we going?"

"We'll be safe near the lake," replied the rabbit. "Follow me."

It was almost nighttime when they reached the lake. Along its shores, the animals Harwinton had seen in the clearing were stretched out on the ground. Some were too exhausted to move while others wearily lifted their heads to see who the newcomers were. As he and Bumper walked by, Harwinton was sure he recognized Pete and Polly Possum who lived in an old hickory tree near the den. Anxiously, the bear strained his to see who else had sought safety here, but no other bears had come to the lake. Maybe Pete and Polly know where my family is, thought Harwinton. I must ask them in the morning.

Finding a soft mound of grass sheltered by two towering pine trees, Harwinton and Bumper lay down to rest. "Our families must be worried about us," said the rabbit, stifling a yawn. "Sure hope nothing's happened to any of them."

"I hope so, too," answered Harwinton.

Bumper was soon fast asleep. For a long time, the young bear lay awake gazing up at the bright moon and starry sky. He remembered a time when he had gone fishing with Poppa. While Harwinton had splashed in the cool water, Poppa had told him a story about how God had created the whole world. But Harwinton had been too busy playing to really pay attention. He wondered where Poppa was now.

"God," whispered Harwinton, his eyelids drooping sleepily, "if you're listening, please let our families be safe."

CHAPTER 3

A Ray of Hope

In the morning, Bumper was the first to wake up. He scrambled to his feet, anxious to find out what had happened to his home and his family.

"Harwinton!" he called.

"What do you want?" mumbled the sleepy bear.

"Get up! It's morning."

Harwinton rolled over, stretched and slowly got up. What a beautiful day! The sky was a brilliant blue. The sun danced merrily on the lake, making pretty sparkles on the water. A tiny, red-faced bird sang loudly from a shady elm tree. But as the bear slowly inhaled the morning air, the hint of stale smoke reminded him of the reason he had slept here instead of in his warm, cozy bed. To his dismay, the Possums, along with the other animals, had already left.

Harwinton and Bumper hurriedly made their way back to where the fire had been. Amazingly, most of the campgrounds had been spared, but when they reached the honeysuckle field, they could hardly believe their eyes! Everywhere they looked, a sooty black had replaced the bright green of summer. Friendly trees surrounding the once-happy field had been reduced to crumbling stumps.

Bumper ran to the burrow he had called home. "Everything's gone!" he cried. Worst of all, there was no sign of his family. "Wait, Harwinton! Where are you going?"

"I have to see my house!"

Reluctant to be left alone, Bumper raced after Harwinton. The path he had so often traveled upon was totally gone now, but instinctively the young bear followed the way.

When at last he reached the den, the sight that met his eyes made him gasp in horror—the thick bushes that had sheltered his home were now a pile of smoldering ashes.

"Momma! Poppa!" he called. No one answered.

Harwinton stepped on something hard. He bent down and found the charred metal rim of the new honey barrel Poppa had made last summer. The tree! Afraid to look, the cub slowly turned around. The tree was still standing.

Just then, they saw two forest rangers scouting

the area. Harwinton and Bumper ran behind the giant tree. From their hiding place, they could hear the two men talking.

"Guess we've found all the animals we're going to find," said the tall, thin one. "The rest must have run off."

"Looks that way," replied his partner. "Say, wasn't there a family of bears living here?"

"Yeah! Seven of 'em."

"Did you check inside the den?"

"Bill did early this morning. There's no trace of 'em. He couldn't find any of the rabbits, either."

"I sure hope they got out in time. Any idea what caused it?"

"Some campers didn't properly extinguish their fire before they left. It's been so dry from the lack of rain, it didn't take much to get a blaze going."

"With all the safety rules and warning signs, you'd think people would be more careful. Well, there's no use looking anymore around here. Where else do we need to go?"

"This is the last place. We'd better report back to the station."

Harwinton and Bumper watched sorrowfully until the two men were out of sight. Was it really true? Were they now orphans? Heartbroken, they held each other and sobbed.

"Our families are gone," wailed Bumper. "We'll

never see them again."

"Yes, we will," insisted Harwinton, wiping his own tears away. "Last night I asked God to keep our families safe and I believe he did. They *must* have gotten away or the rangers would have found them by now."

"Then what are we going to do?" asked the rabbit, drying his eyes.

"We're going to look for them," said Harwinton firmly. "And we won't stop searching until we find them."

"But which way shall we go?"

They looked around at the paths before them. All the trails appeared dark and scary. Which one should they take? Then, as if in answer to Bumper's question, a ray of sunshine broke through the clouds and shed its beam onto the pathway to their right.

"Let's go that way," said Harwinton.

Staying close to each other, they followed the shaft of light down the rocky trail. The cub thought about what the forest rangers had said. It was some campers who had started the fire. Anger began to well up inside him. He decided he would never trust humans. They had destroyed his home.

On the trail, the two friends passed by other animals who had also lost their homes in the fire. "Have you seen the Bear or Rabbit families?" Harwinton or Bumper shouted to them.

"No! Sorry!" came the all-too-familiar answer.

Among the animals they met were Pete and Polly Possum. After missing his chance to talk with them at the lake, Harwinton was relieved to see his neighbors again. The bear eagerly asked them the usual question, hoping this time for a positive answer.

"Polly and I weren't home when the fire started," explained Pete, "and there was no way we could get back there until this morning. We've lost everything, too."

"We can't find my sister and her family, either," added Polly, tears welling up in her eyes. "I'm so worried about them." She looked sympathetically at Harwinton and Bumper. "We'll pray that you find your parents soon."

"Yes," agreed Pete hastily. "Sorry, boys, but Polly and I need to move on. Take good care of yourselves, now. Ya hear?"

"We will," answered Bumper. "Thanks for your help."

"Hope you find your sister," called Harwinton as he waved good-bye.

The Possums had walked only a short distance from them, when Polly's sister and her family emerged from the forest from a different direction. Happily, both families ran to each other. With mixed feelings, Harwinton and Bumper watched them as they hugged and cried. The two friends exchanged wistful looks, while both of them wondered the same thing—would their own search have a similar outcome?

"Pardon me," said a voice unexpectedly. "Could I be of any assistance?"

Harwinton and Bumper turned toward the direction of the sound. Clinging to a branch of a nearby tree was an old hoot owl, his glasses crooked on his pointy beak. The bear eyed the old bird closely. *This* didn't look like one of The Dark Forest owls. This one was bigger and his wings had a gleam to them that none of the other owls had.

"Please allow me to introduce myself," offered the stately old bird, while he adjusted his spectacles. "I am Tobiah T. Owl."

"My name is Harwinton Bear," answered Harwinton. "And this is my friend, Bumper Rabbit."

"How do you do, Harwinton, Bumper," replied Tobiah pleasantly.

Awestruck by the gleaming stranger, Bumper said nothing; he simply stared. Harwinton shook like jelly inside but was not afraid. There was something peaceful and comforting about this powerful-looking bird.

"Excuse me, sir," said the cub, "but I don't remember ever seeing you at the Owl family's house. Do you live in The Dark Forest?"

"No, I come from a forest quite a distance from

here," explained Tobiah. "I am on my way home from a special journey and was hoping to stay the night with a friend of mine when the fire broke out. It was rather frightening, if I do say so myself."

"Y-yes, sir," said the rabbit, still staring at the bird. "Lots of animals lost their homes, including us."

"Why, that's terrible, Bumper," replied Tobiah sadly. "But!" he added, his face brightening, "I believe everything is going to be fine, just wait and see!" The owl smiled and eagerly nodded his head at the young rabbit. Encouraged, Bumper smiled back.

"Have you found your friend, sir?" asked Harwinton.

"No, not yet."

"What's his name?" asked Bumper. "Maybe we've seen him."

"Mr. Barnaby Bat."

Harwinton and Bumper shook their heads.

"That's quite all right," said Tobiah. "Now, who are *you* looking for?"

The owl listened intently to Harwinton and Bumper, then closed his eyes for a few moments. "Oh, dear!" he said with a frown on his face. "There was so much confusion yesterday, what with animals running here and there; that it is difficult for me to remember very clearly."

"We understand," said Harwinton.

"No, now wait a minute," continued Tobiah. "I think I did see a family of bears and rabbits some-time during the fire. In fact, I think they were on this very trail. How I wish I could be of more help to you. I hope you find them."

"So do we," answered the cub. "Thank you, Mr. Owl. Good-bye, sir!"

"Godspeed, my friends!"

Harwinton and Bumper left Tobiah and continued on the sunlit trail. They were silent, each lost in their own thoughts: What had happened to their families?

CHAPTER 4

Danger!

After several days the path Harwinton and Bumper were following turned sharply downward and led them through an eerie, dank thicket of wildly overgrown bushes. The tall, monster-looking trees overhead grew so close together the sunbeam could barely light the way before them. Long, mournful cries from an unseen animal broke the chilling silence surrounding them. The foul smell from a murky swamp clung to the motionless air.

"Let's hurry up out of here," whispered Bumper nervously.

"I'm with you," answered Harwinton.

Straining to walk faster through the creeping vines that covered the ground, they passed by a fallen, hollowed-out tree trunk. Lazily stretched out upon it, seemingly asleep, was a dirty red fox.

"Where are you fellas off to?" he called out pleasantly.

Surprised by the unexpected question, Harwinton and Bumper stopped. A faint, uneasy feeling began to flutter in the bear's tummy.

"We're looking for the Bear and Rabbit families," explained Bumper, turning to answer. "They used to live in The Dark Forest."

"Ah, yes," said the fox, squinting so he could see them better. "There was a big fire there. Well, I have some good news for you. I've seen your families!"

"You have?" exclaimed the two friends. "Where?"

"If you follow the *shorter* path to your left," he whispered, a glint in his beady eyes, "I'm sure you'll meet up with them. I saw them heading that way."

"Oh, thank you so much, Mr. Fox," they cried.

"You're quite welcome," he replied with a toothless grin. "Have a safe trip." In an instant he was gone, disappearing into a hole hidden by the fallen tree trunk.

"Come on, Harwinton!" shouted Bumper, heading toward the other trail. "Let's go! He said to take the shorter path to our left."

Ignoring the uneasy feeling, the young bear started to follow his friend when a strange thing happened. His legs would not move!

"Come on!" shouted Bumper again. "What's the matter?"

Harwinton was standing stock-still. Inside, his fluttery tummy was now doing flip-flops and his heart beat fast with fear. The word 'DANGER' repeatedly flashed across his mind. Could it be his imagination? Or was the sunbeam struggling to shine brighter through the thick ceiling of leaves, as if urging them to stay on the path they were following?

"No, Bumper," answered Harwinton, finally able to speak. "We mustn't go that way."

"But Mr. Fox said..."

"I don't care what he said. I don't trust him. Something is bad about that trail. The sunbeam is still pointing to our right; and that's the way I'm going."

With a determined look on his face, Harwinton marched down the dimly lit path. Frustrated, Bumper ran after him trying to persuade his friend to turn back. But Harwinton would not listen.

"Do what you want then," said Bumper angrily. "I'm taking the other trail." And off he went before Harwinton could stop him.

For several miles, the young bear trudged up a winding steep hill. At the crest of it, he came to a footbridge. The bridge spanned a narrow ravine. At the bottom of the ravine were huge, jagged rocks. I wonder where Bumper is, thought Harwinton.

"Help! Somebody help me!" cried a voice.

Not far off to the left was another footbridge which crossed an even higher part of the ravine. The ropes were undone on one side, and the bridge dangled limply from the brittle stakes to which it had been fastened. Harwinton quickly realized the trail Mr. Fox had said to take led to that very bridge, and the voice had come from that direction.

"I'm coming!" called the bear, racing toward the other bridge. To his horror, when Harwinton looked over the edge, he found Bumper clinging tightly to one of the stakes.

"HELP!" shrieked the terrified rabbit.

"Hold on, Bumper. I'll save you." Lying on his stomach, Harwinton leaned over and held out his paw. "Here! Grab onto me and I'll pull you up."

Bumper tried, but as he did so the stake made a cracking noise. "I'm going to fall!" he screamed. Frozen with fear, he refused to move again.

Just then, a large bird, which had been circling above them, swooped down and grasped Bumper in its claws. "Don't be afraid," said the bird. "I've got you."

Before Bumper knew it, he was safely on the grass. The worst over, he began to sob.

"Mr. Owl!" cried Harwinton.

"At your service," answered Tobiah, his wings

sparkling like an angel's in the sunbeam's rays. "Bumper, how did you ever get into so much trouble?"

"A fox told us he saw our folks take this path," wailed the rabbit. "Harwinton wouldn't follow it, so I got mad and took it anyway. I didn't notice the bridge was out until it was too late. I should've followed the sunbeam."

"Hmm..." hummed the owl thoughtfully. "Tell me, was that fox you spoke to near a fallen tree trunk?"

"Yes!" exclaimed Harwinton. "Why?"

"That sly fellow's name is Pretender. He's known as the biggest taleteller around. There's not an animal in the forest that believes a word he says. Surely you've heard of him?"

"No," answered Harwinton.

"But he said he *saw* our folks go that way," sniffed Bumper.

"My young rabbit," said Tobiah kindly, "there's something else you need to know about Mr. Pretender. He's told so many tales now he can't see straight any more. My guess is he never saw your folks at all. He's almost as blind as a bat—may my friend Barnaby forgive me for saying so."

"Something told me that old fox was lying," said the cub, remembering the warning he had felt inside that had kept him on the right path.

"Why would he do that?" asked Bumper. "I could've..." He stopped, shivering at the thought of what almost happened.

"I guess some animals are just as mean as some people," remarked Harwinton, thinking of the campers who had started the fire.

"Yes, unfortunately that is so," agreed Tobiah, "but you mustn't let it stop *you* from doing what is right."

"Mr. Owl," asked Bumper, looking sadly at the bridge, "what if our folks...?" His voice trailed off and he started to sob again.

"Little friend," answered Tobiah gently, "don't think about the 'what ifs' once you know the truth. The important thing for you to do now is to keep searching. You never know when the very thing you are hoping for will happen."

"You're right, Mr. Owl," said Harwinton. "We're not giving up. Are you okay now, Bumper?"

"I-I guess so," replied the rabbit in a shaky voice. "But that sure was a close one."

Before going on their way, Harwinton and Bumper, under Tobiah's direction, managed to roll a large, dead tree limb across the path to the fallen bridge. Then they piled rocks and branches all around it as a further warning to others of the danger.

"Fine work, boys!" exclaimed Tobiah, flapping his wings for takeoff. "I'll be going now. Good journey to you."

"So long, Mr. Owl," called Harwinton and Bumper. "And thank you!"

They watched until Tobiah was out of sight. The bright sunbeam pierced through the shady trees and lighted the way to the good bridge. Slowly, the two friends picked their way across it. "Sunbeam," whispered Harwinton, when they had safely reached the other side, "I'm sure glad you're with us."

CHAPTER 5

The Shaded Forest

Later that afternoon, Harwinton and Bumper came upon an old, gnarled maple tree. Hanging on the tree was a roughly cut piece of wood with faded writing on it.

"Can you make out what this sign says?" asked the rabbit.

" 'Welcome to The Shaded Forest,' " slowly read the bear. "This sign looks like it was made a long time ago. I wonder if anybody's around."

Just beyond the maple tree was a pond. Realizing how thirsty they were, they ran to the edge and took a long, hearty drink of the cool water. Across from where they were, Bumper noticed a huge pile of sticks. "Harwinton, look over there. What's that for?"

"Let's go see."

Harwinton led the way while Bumper stayed close behind him. After what had happened with Mr. Pretender, the young rabbit wasn't taking any more chances. They could hear a chomping noise as they crept closer to the huge pile of sticks. Crouching down, Harwinton stopped at the edge of a crop of tall grass and peeked out. There, on the bank of the pond, sat two young beavers, their open dinner pail beside them.

"We'll be done with the new dam soon!" Harwinton heard the smaller one say.

"Yes!" replied the second. "Say! Did you hear something?"

Just then, a blade of grass tickled Bumper's nose. "ACH-CHOO!" He sneezed so hard he lost his balance and fell against Harwinton, pushing the cub forward. Out tumbled the bear followed by a surprised, wide-eyed rabbit. Harwinton and Bumper landed a few feet from the equally surprised beavers.

"Uh-can we help you, sonnies?" lisped the bigger beaver.

"Please excuse us," replied Harwinton, getting up quickly and dusting himself off.

"We're trying to find our families," explained Bumper, pulling a piece of grass from his tail. "We got separated from them during the fire."

"That's too bad," answered the bigger beaver.

"We heard the fire was pretty serious. Many of the animals from The Dark Forest have come here to live. Maybe your folks did, too. You're welcome to stay with the Mrs. and me while you look for them. My name is Woody and this is my wife, Wilhelmina. What are your names?"

Harwinton and Bumper introduced themselves. Needing time to rest, they decided to accept Woody's invitation. Mrs. Beaver knew most of the families who had come from their part of the forest. "I'll take you to visit them," she promised. "Perhaps one of them will know something about your folks."

For two weeks, the young bear and rabbit stayed with the Beavers. Everyday they went with Wilhelmina to talk with a different Dark Forest family. But the results were always the same—everyone had been in such a hurry to escape from the fire, they hadn't noticed either the Bears or the Rabbits.

One afternoon they visited a field mouse named PeppyRoni. Peppy was from a far-away country called Italy. With great interest, Harwinton, Bumper and Wilhelmina listened while the mouse told how he had made the long journey on a big cargo ship. During the day, he would hide among the huge crates to avoid being caught. Then at night, when most of the crew was asleep, Peppy would search the ship for whatever crumbs of food he could find. After many weeks, the ship finally docked and Peppy left to find a new home. He had only lived a short time in The Dark Forest before the fire.

"Now, tella me your story," he said, nodding to his guests.

Harwinton and Bumper each took turns talking about what had happened to them and described their families to him. "Do you remember seeing any of the bears or rabbits that day?" asked the cub.

PeppyRoni thought and thought as he rocked back and forth atop the tree stump he was sitting on. Slowly he shook his head. "I'ma so sorry!' he squeaked. "I wish I coulda helpa you." Big tears began to roll down the emotional mouse's cheeks. "It'sa so sadda!" he sniffed. "Poor bambinos gotta no family."

"Hush, Peppy," whispered Mrs. Beaver. "The boys feel bad enough as it is."

Pulling out a big red-and-white-checkered hand-kerchief, Peppy loudly blew his nose. "*Scusa* me, you righta."

"I guess we'd better be going," said Wilhelmina. "It's almost time for Woody to be home and I must get supper ready. Thank you, Peppy. Good day now."

The walk back to the pond seemed much longer this time. "Are there any more families left on your list, Mrs. Beaver?" asked Harwinton hopefully, when they had arrived at the dam.

"No, dear," she answered gently. "I wish there were, but PeppyRoni was the last one."

After supper, Bumper and Harwinton told the Beavers of their decision to leave the next morning to continue their search. Mrs. Beaver wanted them to stay. "We could help you build a place close to us," she said.

"Thank you," answered Harwinton. "You've both been so kind, but I must keep looking. You can stay if you want to, Bumper."

"No, I want to keep looking, too. Besides, I can't let you go alone."

Very early the next morning, Mrs. Beaver packed food in a bright red cloth and tied it shut. To help Harwinton and Bumper carry it, Woody gnawed off a smooth stick from a hickory tree and slid the bundle onto it.

"Have a safe trip," he lisped. "And remember, you're always welcome to come back here."

"Thanks, Woody," they answered.

PeppyRoni happened by and heard the news that Harwinton and Bumper were leaving. The little mouse scurried off to tell all the animals so they could come and wish their new friends well on their journey. Peppy then followed Harwinton and Bumper to the entrance of The Shaded Forest. He watched, alternately waving his red-and-white handkerchief and drying his eyes, until the bear and rabbit were out of sight.

CHAPTER 6

The Thunderstorm

Much to Harwinton and Bumper's delight, the sunbeam returned as they passed by the old, gnarled maple tree with the faded sign. The beam of light led them down a trail that was well-marked and comfortable to walk on.

Shuffling their way through a pile of dead leaves, the glint of a shiny object caught Harwinton's eye. Stooping to pick it up, he cried out to his friend. "Bumper! Come here! Look at this!"

The rabbit turned around. "What have you found?"

In Harwinton's paw was a silver pocket-watch. "It looks like my Poppa's!" exclaimed the bear. Quickly turning it over, Harwinton anxiously searched for the familiar inscription. There it was:

To Our Poppa, With Love.

"Bumper! *It is his!* We gave it to him for his birthday last year."

"Maybe they're not far ahead of us," added Bumper eagerly.

In their excitement, the two friends raced off, leaving the sunbeam behind. Stopping now and then, they called out their families' names. Anxiously they waited, listening hard for an answer. But none came. For an hour they searched, getting farther and farther away from the well-marked trail. Harwinton realized it was getting late.

"Bumper, let's go back before we get lost," he said.

"I guess we'd better," answered the rabbit. "This isn't working. Let's see. We came frommm—that direction."

It looked the same, but after a short distance, the trail they had chosen abruptly ended. Thick bushes and tall grass blocked what should have been the path.

"*Now* which way do we go?" cried Bumper fearfully.

Harwinton was confused, too. Which path was the right one? And where was the sunbeam? "I don't know, Bumper," he answered, wishing they hadn't been so foolish.

Tired and hungry, they decided to sit down and

rest. While they ate the last of the food Mrs. Beaver had packed for them, the sky grew black and threatening. The distant grumbling of thunder was growing louder.

"We'd better run for cover, Bumper," said Harwinton. "It looks like a big storm's coming."

They had barely wriggled their way under some heavy brush, when a drenching rain started to fall. A fierce wind arose. Whipping angrily through the trees, it snapped off branches and hurled them at the young bear and rabbit. Soggy leaves blew about in all directions, dropping for a moment to the ground before being twirled away through the air again.

Suddenly, a terrifying bolt of lightning struck a tree near where Harwinton and Bumper were hiding. The tree, already swaying helplessly in the strong wind, began to fall directly towards the two frightened animals.

"LOOK OUT!" they screamed.

Briars and blowing branches scratched at them as they tore through the brush and thick grass. Safely out of the way of the falling tree, they dropped to the ground gasping for air. Glancing up, Harwinton saw an opening in a large pile of rocks.

"Let's hide in there!" he shouted to Bumper.

With their last ounce of energy, they crawled up the sides of the rocks and into the opening. Snug and dry inside the shelter, they could still hear the howling wind and the torrential beating of the rain on the leaves. Little by little the thunder and lightning died down. It was night when the storm finally stopped and all was quiet. The glow of the full moon illuminated the sky and trickled its way through the opening in the rocks.

"Harwinton, your paw is hurt," exclaimed Bumper, now able to see his friend in the moon's light.

"You have a bump on your head, Bump."

Both of them started to giggle. It sounded funny—Bump had a bump.

"We'll stay here for the night and try to find the trail tomorrow," said the cub. "Maybe the sunbeam will be out there to show us the way."

"Harwinton," said Bumper, "don't you think we should go back to the Beavers?"

"But the watch..."

"Just because you found it doesn't mean our families are all right. Besides, are you sure it's your Poppa's?"

"I'm sure," answered Harwinton firmly. "It has the writing on it. Look! I'll show you."

Harwinton went to reach for the cloth Mrs. Beaver had wrapped the food in. Where had he put it? "Bumper, do you have the bundle? I put the watch in it after we ate."

"Uh-uh! I thought *you* had it."

"Oh, no!" cried the bear. "We must have left it behind when the tree started to fall."

"There's no use going back to look for it; we'd never find it now," said the rabbit. "And maybe we'd better give up looking for our folks, too. We're not getting anywhere."

Harwinton knew Bumper was right, but something inside him told him not to give up yet. "Let's keep looking just a little longer. I still believe we'll find them."

"Well—okay. But just a little longer."

Exhausted from all the excitement of the day, they were soon fast asleep, unaware of the unusual turn their journey was about to take.

CHAPTER 7

The City of Light

Click! The front door of the brown, two-story house closed quietly behind the children.

"There they are!" exclaimed Susie Stevenson, her short, dark hair bouncing as she skipped away to catch up with her friends.

"Hey! Wait for us," called her older brother, Johnny, who was quickly tying his sneakers. "Come on, Ben. Come on, Michael. They're leaving. Let's go!"

"Race all of ya to the field," challenged eight-year old, freckle-faced Danny.

"Last one there's a turtle," sang out red-haired Mitsi as she dashed off toward the hill. Laughing, the other children followed after her.

Golden rays from the sunbeam filtered into the

shelter where Harwinton and Bumper were still fast asleep. Curled up in a corner, the small rabbit happily thumped a hind foot to the beat of the beautiful music. *Music?* Bumper woke with a start. He hadn't been dreaming. The distinct sound of music echoed around and through the shelter.

"Harwinton," he cried, shaking his friend. "Wake up! Listen!"

"What is it?" yawned the bear, rubbing his eyes.

"Somebody's singing out there."

Harwinton sat up. Somebody *was* singing! But where were they? Looking around, he noticed another opening to the shelter. Where did this one go? Motioning Bumper to follow, they slowly crept toward it. The closer they came to the other side, the louder the singing grew.

"Bumper," whispered Harwinton excitedly. "Are we in heaven? Listen to the words."

"Oh, be quiet," answered the rabbit impatiently, wishing more than ever he'd stayed with the Beavers. "We can't be *that* lost."

Cautiously, they looked out. To their surprise, The Shaded Forest had ended and stretching out before them was the greenest meadow they had ever seen. Beautiful flowers dotted the grass with lovely shades of blue, white and yellow.

Grabbing a reluctant Bumper by the paw, Harwinton pulled him to a nearby tree to get a closer look at the source of the lively music. Dancing and singing together in the meadow was a group of children. Their tune was such a joyful one, the cub immediately started swaying to the music. This is the song the children were singing:

*Papa God's Rainbow up in the sky—Tells
me He loves me, and this is why:
He sent Jesus for me to die. Now He lives
forever way up on high!
Sing Alleluia! Praise to the Lord! Sing
Alleluia! Now and forevermore!
Papa God's Rainbow up in the sky—Tells
me He loves me, and this is why:
He sent Jesus—King is He! And someday
I'll reign with Him—eternally!
Sing Alleluia! Praise to the Lord! Sing
Alleluia! Now and forevermore!
Sing Alleluia! Praise to the Lord! Sing
Alleluia! Now and forevermore!*

Harwinton listened closely to the words. While he knew what a rainbow was, the song talked about things that were totally new to him. *Papa* God? His own Poppa had told him about God, but Harwinton had never heard him called Papa before. And who was Jesus?

By the end of the song, Bumper was really

scared. "Harwinton, let's get out of here."

"Bumper, there's no need to be afraid. Bumper! Wait! Come back!"

The children had quieted down and were picking the pretty flowers. One of the young boys, Johnny, heard a rustling noise. Quickly turning around, he saw a bear cub running after a rabbit and disappearing into an opening behind some trees. Signaling to the others, Johnny slowly followed in the direction the animals had gone. Peering into the opening of the shelter, he saw two pairs of frightened eyes.

"Look!" loudly whispered Johnny's sister. "A little bear and bunny!"

"Shh, Susie, you'll scare them," said Johnny. Softly, he called to the animals. "Come on out. We won't hurt you. Are you hungry?"

Both Harwinton and Bumper realized their tummies were feeling empty. Come to think of it, they hadn't eaten since yesterday.

"Oh!" cried Mitsi. "The poor bunny has a bump on his head."

"Yeah! And one of the bear's paws is hurt, too," added Michael.

"This calls for Ben and Danny's ambulance service," said Johnny.

"Gotchya!" chorused the two brothers as they raced home to get their red wagons.

Too tired to run anymore, Harwinton and Bumper allowed the children to place one of them in each of the wagons. Making siren sounds, the children took turns pulling the wagons along the path that weaved its way through the meadow. When Harwinton glanced up to see where they were going, shining its light ahead of them was the sunbeam. How much brighter it shone here.

As they passed a mighty oak tree, a soft hooting sound made Harwinton turn his head. That bird dozing on one of the branches—could it be? Just then, the bird briefly opened his eyes and winked at Harwinton. It was Tobiah T. Owl! They had not seen him since he had rescued Bumper that awful day near the ravine. What's he doing here? wondered the young bear to himself as he stared at the snoring bird.

"Where are we taking them?" asked Mitsi, as she took another turn pulling one of the wagons.

"To our house," answered Johnny. "Dad's an animal doctor. He'll know what to do for them."

When they came to the end of the meadow, nestled at the bottom of a gently sloping hill was the city where the children lived. In the distance, Harwinton could see tall buildings, their roofs gleaming in the bright sunshine.

The wagons bumped and jostled as the children raced down the hill. Ben and Danny ran on ahead to get Johnny's and Susie's dad.

"Dr. Stevenson! Dr. Stevenson!" they shouted. "Come quick!"

Dr. John Stevenson soon appeared at the door. A tall, dark-haired man, he had been a veterinarian for ten years now. "What's the matter?" he called.

"Look what we've found, Dad," answered Johnny. "They're hurt. Can you help them?"

"Sure," said the doctor, when he saw the animals in the wagons. "Bring them around to the back door of my office."

The children brought Harwinton and Bumper into the large, neat, shiny-clean room. Along one white-painted wall stood a large, wooden cabinet filled with bandages and small bottles of medicines. Opposite the cabinet was a sink, where Dr. Stevenson was busy washing his hands. While Johnny and Michael gently lifted Harwinton onto the long table that stood in the middle of the room, the doctor examined Bumper's bump.

"Praise God!" he said. "It's nothing serious, Mister Rabbit. We'll have you fixed up in no time."

Bumper had never been called Mister before. He decided he liked Dr. Stevenson, especially when he gave the little rabbit a juicy carrot to nibble on while he looked at Harwinton's paw.

As he worked, the doctor talked happily, dotting his sentences with a "Praise God" here and a "Praise the Lord" there. What kind of people *are* these?

quietly wondered Harwinton. They are being nice to us, but I don't trust them. Remembering it had been humans who had destroyed his home, the young bear decided to stay only as long as it took to get well. Then he and Bumper would be on their way.

"Johnny and Susie, run and tell your mother we have houseguests," said Dr. Stevenson as he put the bandages back on the shelf.

"Yes, Dad!"

A few minutes later, they returned with Mrs. Stevenson and their two-year-old sister, Joy. Mrs. Stevenson gave Harwinton and Bumper a warm, friendly smile.

"How adorable," she exclaimed. "Where did you find them?"

"The children told me they were playing in the meadow when Johnny heard a noise," answered the doctor. "The animals were hiding in the old rock cave."

"Are they badly hurt, John?"

"No, but we need to take care of them for a few days until they can be set free."

"I wonder how they got here," said Mrs. Stevenson.

"I'll call the ranger station at The Lighted Forest. Perhaps two of their animals are lost." Dr. Stevenson dialed the number and put the receiver on a small machine that looked like a typewriter. He typed for several minutes before hanging up. "Now that's interesting," said the doctor as he turned off the small machine.

"What's wrong, Daddy?" asked Susie.

"Ranger Goodwill said all of their animals are accounted for. But he told me there was a very bad fire about a month ago at another wildlife park. He wondered if maybe these two are from there."

"Did he know the name of the other park?" asked Mrs. Stevenson.

"Yes. He said it was The Dark Forest."

Johnny's eyes widened in disbelief. "Dad! That's miles away from here!"

"I know, son," answered the doctor. "These two have been traveling a long time. You get more food and I'll prepare a place for them to sleep in here."

Mrs. Stevenson motioned for Susie and Joy to follow her. "Supper's almost ready, John. Will you be much longer?"

"No, just a few minutes more."

Dr. Stevenson found two big cages, cleaned them and set them up in a warm, sunny corner of the room. Johnny soon returned with two plates of food. For Bumper, there were lettuce leaves and more juicy carrots. For Harwinton, there was fish and lots of sweet honey. It looked so good!

"You know, Johnny," remarked Dr. Stevenson, "they seem pretty tame for forest animals. I think I'll leave the cage doors open until bedtime. Come on, let's go eat."

The Stevenson's kitchen was next to the room where Harwinton and Bumper were. Through the swinging doors they heard Susie exclaim, "Daddy! We're supposed to thank Jesus first!"

Harwinton and Bumper stopped eating and looked at each other. "Thank *WHO*?" asked Bumper, quickly swallowing a lettuce leaf.

"I don't know, but if they're praying we'd better be polite and do as they do," replied the bear.

Both animals bowed their heads, each keeping one eye peeking at the plates of food before them.

"It's my turn to pray, Dad," said Johnny from the other room.

"Go ahead, then."

"Dear Papa God," prayed Johnny, "thank you for this food. Thank you for helping us find the little bear and rabbit; and please show us where they live. In Jesus' name. Amen."

"Is it okay to eat *now*?" asked Bumper.

"I guess so," answered Harwinton. The two animals nibbled quietly so they could hear the Stevensons talking.

"Daddy, do you think Jesus led them here to The City of Light?" asked Susie.

"I'm sure of it," he answered. Turning to Mrs. Stevenson he added, "After we eat, I'll try to call the ranger station at The Dark Forest. Hope someone there can tell me where those animals belong."

"We've told everybody we've met about our families," muttered Bumper bitterly, "and no one's been able to help us. What makes him think he can?"

"Ssh, let's listen to what they're saying!"

"I hope so, too, John," replied Mrs. Stevenson. "But remember, by ourselves we can't do anything. We need to pray for wisdom."

Bumper made a face at that. "Now what good is that going to do?"

"Bumper, we've tried everything else," said Harwinton. "What do we have to lose?"

"Well," answered the rabbit, "they can do that if they want to, but I want to go back to The Shaded Forest."

A few hours later, joyful sounds drifted up to them from another part of the house. Curious to know what it was, Harwinton eagerly pawed at the door of his cage. To his surprise it flew open. Dr. Stevenson had forgotten to lock it. The cub easily pushed through the swinging doors that led to the kitchen. Following the sound, he quietly walked down a hallway and came to the top of a staircase. In the room below sat Dr. and Mrs. Stevenson with a group of their friends. Some of the people were singing in different languages, while others were praying silently. Finding his cage was also unlocked, Bumper crept out and stood next to Harwinton.

"What are they doing down there?" asked the rabbit in a hushed tone of voice.

"They're singing something, but I can't understand the words."

"I don't know about these people, Harwinton. They seem nice, but they sure are weird."

"They just really believe in God, Bumper, that's all."

"Well, I don't," angrily whispered the rabbit. "He took our families away."

"That's not true! Don't say things like that."

They stopped their conversation and listened to the prayers the Stevensons and their friends were saying.

"Hey," whispered Bumper excitedly. "They are praying for us. You don't suppose that stuff is really going to work, do you?"

"We could stay around awhile and see," suggested Harwinton.

"Oh, all right," sighed Bumper. "But after this, I give up. Okay?"

"Okay."

The cub lay awake for a long time thinking about everything he had seen and heard that day. All kinds of questions had been doing somersaults in his mind. Now, there was a new one. What had Susie meant about Jesus—there was that name again—leading them to The City of Light? The word 'Light' caused

Harwinton to remember the bright sunbeam that had been with them through The Dark and The Shaded Forests. Where had that light come from, anyway? Had God sent it?

"I must ask Poppa," murmured Harwinton as he slowly drifted off to sleep.

CHAPTER 8

Ranger George

The next morning, Johnny, Susie and Joy burst into the room while the animals were still sleeping. Dr. Stevenson, who had been reading the morning paper, followed after them. "Be quiet, children," he ordered. "Let them rest. Now go and play, please."

The older children did as they were told; but when no one was looking, Joy snuck back into the office. Approaching one of the cages, she reached in with her small, chubby fingers to touch Harwinton's thick, brown fur. When the cub unexpectedly stretched and sat up, the little girl quickly pulled her hand away. For a few moments one pair of big blue eyes peered into a pair of small, sleepy black ones. From the kitchen next door, came the sound of bacon sizzling. A delicious aroma soon filled the doctor's office.

"Beckfast?" asked Joy.

At the smell of food, both Bumper and Harwinton were awake in a hurry.

"Mommy! Mommy!" cried the little girl as she ran from the room.

"What is it, Joy?" asked Mrs. Stevenson.

"Hungry!" she answered, pointing to the animals in the other room.

Dr. Stevenson laughed at his tiny daughter's expression. "Would you like to help me feed them?" he asked. Joy eagerly nodded and followed him back into the office.

The doctor quickly filled two bowls with food and placed them on the floor beside the cages. When he knelt down to unlatch the doors, he discovered they were partly open. "Hmm, guess I forgot to lock them last night," he murmured to himself.

"John," called Mrs. Stevenson, "I need to go shopping today and won't be here to watch them. Please make sure the cages are fastened. I don't want them to get loose in the house."

"Okay, dear," he answered.

"Me, Daddy!" insisted Joy, picking up one of the bowls from the floor.

"All right. But don't drop it now."

Giggling excitedly, Joy carefully placed one dish

in each cage. Shyly, she petted Bumper. "Soft," she whispered.

"Yes, I know," answered Dr. Stevenson, as he checked Bumper's bump. "You look much better today, Mister Rabbit. Now, let's look at Mr. Bear." The doctor examined Harwinton's paw. "He's doing fine, too, but I'll put some more medicine on it just to make sure no infection gets in there."

When he was finished, Dr. Stevenson locked the cages and cleaned up. "We'd better get you ready, Joy. Your Mommy wants to leave soon."

"You come, too, Daddy?"

"No, honey. Daddy has to go see someone about getting the animals back home."

"Stay here?"

"No, honey, we can't keep them. They need to live in a place where they can run and play and roam free."

Little Joy looked sad as she followed her Daddy out of the room. "Bye, bye!" she called, waving to the bear and rabbit.

When the door had closed, Bumper lost no time in starting to eat.

"Wait, Bumper!" whispered Harwinton. "We're supposed to pray first, remember?"

"But we did that *last* night," protested his friend.

"Bumperrr..."

"Oh, all right," sighed the rabbit. "Thank you,

God, for this food. Amen."

Dr. Stevenson turned onto the narrow, paved road that led to the Ranger Station. In a few minutes he stopped in front of the small trailer that served as the office. A tall, bearded, gray-haired man came to the door. Ranger George Goodwill looked the same as any other person, yet he was different: a childhood illness had caused him to lose his hearing. While he was able to speak, he often preferred to communicate in Sign Language, the language of the Deaf. Ranger Goodwill had a special gift of working with animals and he communicated his love and concern for them the same way he did with everyone—with his hands and facial expressions. Dr. Stevenson had learned George's language and enjoyed conversing with this funny and godly man.

"Hello, George," signed Dr. Stevenson. "How are you?"

"Good Morning," George signed back. "I'm fine. What's up?"

"I need to get in touch with the ranger station at The Dark Forest. Do you have their phone number? I thought I had it and tried calling them yesterday, but there was no answer."

"Oh, I see," answered George. "Yes, I have it. It's been changed. Coffee?"

"Yes. Thanks."

While Ranger George looked up the number, Dr.

Stevenson sat down at the table and took a sip from the hot, steaming cup.

"Here," signed George as he handed the doctor a piece of paper.

"Wonderful! Thank you so much."

"How are those animals doing?"

"Very well," answered Dr. Stevenson. "I'm planning to have them shipped back to The Dark Forest soon."

"Good," signed George. "But why send them back to The Dark Forest? Why not bring them here?"

"I thought they would do better in their old home."

"The fire destroyed most of the forest," explained George. "There's not much of a home for them to go back to."

"I didn't know that," said Dr. Stevenson.

From a pile of old newspapers on the table, Ranger George pulled out a copy of The Woodlands Gazette and handed it to the doctor to read. The front page held a lengthy article about the fire and some photographs of the destruction.

"How terrible," signed Dr. Stevenson, pointing to the pictures.

George nodded. "The Dark Forest Rangers haven't been able to find any of the bears or rabbits that lived there. If they got out in time, they haven't returned."

Dr. Stevenson sadly shook his head. "Then I have two orphans sitting in my office," he signed. "You're right, George. There's no use sending them back. But will you have room for them here?"

"Of course! God always makes room for the lost," said George. "Bring them whenever they're ready."

"Thanks," answered Dr. Stevenson, getting up to leave. "I guess I won't be needing the phone number now."

"Take it anyway," signed George. "Maybe you should call them to make sure the report hasn't changed."

"Okay, I will. Good-bye! See you soon!"

"Bye. Take care of yourself. Tell your family 'hello' for me."

"You, too. Say 'hello' to Betty for me."

Dr. Stevenson eased the car out of the driveway and back onto the narrow, paved road. On the way to the main highway he noticed a family of bears feeding among the trees. "I hope you'll accept one more," he said to himself as he drove past them.

After supper that evening, as he helped his wife with the dishes, Dr. Stevenson talked about his visit with Ranger Goodwill.

"You mean none of the bears or rabbits survived the fire?" asked Mrs. Stevenson.

"It seems that way," answered the doctor. "I called The Dark Forest station this afternoon. The ranger I spoke with told me they gave up searching for them a long time ago."

"Then what are we going to do, John?"

"Ranger George says they have plenty of room, so I guess the only solution is to bring the animals to The Lighted Forest."

"The poor things," said Mrs. Stevenson. "But The Lighted Forest is a lovely place. I'm sure they'll do just fine there."

"I hope so," sighed Dr. Stevenson wearily. "I'd better go upstairs and tell the kids. Then I'm going to bed. It's been a long day."

Bumper and Harwinton lay quietly in their cages, their plates of food untouched. Tears fell from their eyes as they listened to every word the Stevensons were saying. They had come so far and through so much and now this.

"I knew all that praying wouldn't work," sobbed Bumper. "I told you, Harwinton, God took our families away!"

"He did not!" insisted the bear, remembering the prayer he had said that terrible day of the fire. "They have to be all right. They just have to be."

It was late into the night before either of them could finally settle down. What were they going to do now? Where would they find a home?

CHAPTER 9

The Escape

The next morning, Dr. Stevenson checked Harwinton and Bumper's wounds.

"Are they better, Daddy?" asked Susie.

"Yes, they are. But they didn't touch their food last night. I hope that's not a sign something else is wrong."

"Do you think they know their families are gone?"

Dr. Stevenson paused for a moment and looked at his daughter. "You are a smart little girl," he said, giving her a hug. "It's quite possible they can sense it. I think the time has come to move them to The Lighted Forest. They need to be with their own kind."

"When will we take them?"

"I'll call Ranger George now and make the arrangements."

Susie knelt near the cages. "I'll miss you little bear and bunny," she whispered. "But I know you'll be happy in your new home. Don't worry, Jesus will take care of you."

Dr. Stevenson returned. "It's all set. We'll take them this afternoon after lunch. Okay, Susie, let's leave them alone for awhile. Maybe they'll eat something."

When the door to the office had closed softly behind them, Bumper quickly turned around to face Harwinton's cage. "Did you hear that? They're taking us to that Lighted place."

"I heard," answered the bear.

"Well, I won't stay. I don't even want to go. I want to go back to The Shaded Forest."

"Maybe it won't be so bad, Bumper. There'll be other bears and rabbits there."

"No!" snapped the rabbit. "I've listened to you long enough. Either we go back together or we say good-bye."

Harwinton felt torn. Bumper was the only friend he had and yet he didn't want to live in The Shaded Forest. Feeling defeated, Harwinton nodded. "Okay, we'll go back together."

"Good," said the rabbit. "Let's think of a way out of here."

Both animals thought and thought. "I have an idea," said Harwinton. "We could let them drop us off at The Lighted Forest and leave from there."

"Oh, no you don't," answered Bumper. "If I know you, you'll start to like the place and want to stay. Besides, we don't know how far away it is. We could find our way back to the meadow from here."

"I guess you're right," agreed the cub. "But how will we get loose? Dr. Stevenson will have the cages locked."

Bumper scratched his head with his paw. Suddenly his eyes brightened and his nose began to twitch excitedly. "I have it!" he exclaimed. "When the doctor comes to get us, I'll pretend I'm sick. While he's checking me, you act like you're upset— you know, growl, rattle the door and all that other bear stuff. He'll have to put me down to see what's going on with you. When he does, I'll make a run for it and you follow."

"That won't work!" argued Harwinton. "Do you think he'll open the door if I'm acting like that? He won't want to come near me."

"Well, do you have a better idea?" retorted Bumper.

"No."

"Then at least let's give mine a try."

"Okay, but don't blame me if we end up at The Lighted Forest."

"Ssh! Here he comes now."

Dr. Stevenson entered the room followed by Mrs. Stevenson and two strangers. One was a tall, bearded gray-haired man and the other a pretty, white-haired woman.

"Here they are," signed Dr. Stevenson to the two strangers. "We appreciate your coming here to help us."

"No problem," answered the gray-haired man. "Glad to do it."

Harwinton was so fascinated as he watched the two men converse with their hands, that he forgot to start growling. Meanwhile, Bumper lay in his cage trying to look sick and trying to get Harwinton's attention.

"Betty, do you think you and Mrs. Stevenson can manage the rabbit's cage?" asked the gray-haired man.

"Maybe," she signed back. "Let's try it."

The two women each took one side of the cage and easily lifted it off the floor. "John, we'll be fine," said Mrs. Stevenson, as Betty nodded to the tall man.

"Good!" answered the doctor. "You two bring the rabbit out to George's truck. We'll follow with the cub."

Betty and Mrs. Stevenson slowly walked to the back entrance of the doctor's office. "Johnny!" called Mrs. Stevenson. "Would you open the door, please?"

"Sure, Mom!"

Out the door and around the corner of the house, the two women carried Bumper. As they placed the cage down on the back of the truck, Betty glanced at the rabbit.

"Something's wrong with him," she signed.

Mrs. Stevenson bent down to look at Bumper. Where earlier he had been sitting up, he now lay on his side. His breathing was slow and labored. "You're right!" she signed quickly to Betty. "John! Come here, please. The rabbit's sick."

The two men put Harwinton's cage on the ground. "What's the matter, Mister Rabbit?" asked Dr. Stevenson, as he approached the truck. "You were doing fine yesterday. Don't you want to go to a nice new home?"

When the doctor gently lifted Bumper out of the cage to examine him more closely, Harwinton remembered his part. He began to growl fiercely and show his teeth. Then with all his might, he threw his body against the door of the cage several times.

"What's wrong with the cub?" exclaimed the doctor. Ranger Goodwill moved toward Harwinton to check on him. SNAP! went the bear's teeth.

"I don't believe this, John," cried Mrs. Stevenson. "They've been so calm."

"Here, hold the rabbit," said Dr. Stevenson.

"George, are you all right?"

With all his strength, Harwinton gave one last lunge against the already weakened door hinges. Suddenly, the cage sprang open and the bear tumbled out onto the driveway. Finding himself free, Harwinton raced toward the street.

"Get him!" screamed Mrs. Stevenson, as Bumper leaped from her arms and followed after his friend.

The four adults began frantically chasing after the two animals. Thinking it was a game, Joy, who was sitting in her stroller, clapped her hands and laughed. From inside the house, Johnny and Susie heard the commotion and came running to the front door.

"Johnny, call the police!" shouted Dr. Stevenson. "Susie, take care of Joy!"

Faster and harder, Harwinton and Bumper ran through backyards, swing sets and neatly planted gardens. "My marigolds!" cried an elderly woman. "They've ruined my marigolds!"

Picking up the scent of the strange animals, the neighborhood dogs began to bark while some joined the chase. Harwinton noticed a fence leading to a woodsy area. Running alongside it with Bumper close behind, the cub spotted a break in the railings and dashed through it.

"We've lost them, John," gasped Mrs. Stevenson, stopping to catch her breath.

"They can't get too far," answered the doctor.

"The police will find them and pick them up, I hope. Where's George and Betty?"

"Over there," answered Mrs. Stevenson, pointing to the part of the fence through which the animals had escaped.

"You two okay?" signed the doctor.

"Yes," answered George.

Johnny came running up. "What happened, Dad?"

"I don't know, son. Those animals just went crazy on us. Did you call the police?"

"Yes."

"Good. Thank you. I'd better go down to the station and give them a complete report. They'll have to keep a look out for them."

"Do you think the animals will be all right?" asked Johnny. "I'd hate to see anything bad happen to them."

"Me too, son. We'll have to pray that God will protect them."

Dr. Stevenson motioned for the others to follow him back to the house. On the way, he explained what he needed to do.

"I'll go with you to the police station," said Ranger George.

"Thanks," answered the doctor. "Betty can stay here and rest."

"John?" asked Mrs. Stevenson. "Could you bring

home a pizza? I don't think I have the energy to cook supper tonight."

"Sure, honey. We've all had enough excitement for one day. Let's go, George."

CHAPTER 10

A Trip to the City

Unmindful of the direction in which they were heading, Harwinton and Bumper kept running deeper and deeper into the wooded area. Finally, exhausted and unable to go any farther, they forced themselves to stop and rest for a while.

"Well, I hope you're happy," panted the bear. "You wanted to escape."

"The meadow can't be far from here," said Bumper. "Once we reach the big rock again, we can stay there for the night; then tomorrow start back to The Shaded Forest."

Too tired to answer, Harwinton nodded. An uneasy feeling began to flutter inside his tummy. The same one he had felt that day when they had met the fox named Pretender.

"You ready to move on?" asked Bumper.

"Ready if you are," answered the bear, desperately trying to ignore the warning he was getting. "You lead the way."

Bumper thought for a minute. "The houses are over that way and the meadow was behind them. This path looks right."

Confidently, the rabbit started out, his friend following. They walked for what seemed like hours, but no green meadow came into view. The path led to a paved area and across from that—more trees. Not looking where he was going, Bumper stepped out and onto the hard, black surface. Suddenly, the sound of a blaring horn followed by the squeal of rubber filled the rabbit's ears.

"Watch out, Bumper!" screamed Harwinton as he grabbed for his friend to pull him back.

Somehow the car stopped in time, narrowly missing them. Harwinton glanced up at the human sitting behind the wheel. An odd look of relief and anger was on the man's face. Then, shaking his head and his fist at them, he drove quickly away.

"Thanks, Harwinton," said Bumper, his body shaking from fright. "You saved my life."

"You're welcome," answered the bear, a little impatiently. "But will you please watch where you're going?"

They safely crossed to the other side and walked

past more trees. The dirt path changed to a gravel one. As they followed it, more green began to appear on the ground.

"Look!" cried Bumper. "Grass! The meadow's just ahead of us!"

Excited, they started to run, happy to see a familiar place. How cool and soft the grass felt on their hot, sore feet. Harwinton dropped to the ground and playfully sniffed at the pretty red flowers, while Bumper nibbled on some sweet clover. Yet something felt different. Puzzled, the bear stopped and looked around. There were flowers and trees, but the big rock was nowhere in sight.

A swishing sound caught the cub's attention. Turning his head in its direction, he saw cars and trucks whizzing past. He and Bumper were not in the meadow, but in a park near the busy Main Street in the City of Light. On the sidewalk, people were hurrying by. Some carried packages or led small children by the hand; while others disappeared into tall buildings with big windows.

No longer hungry, Bumper stopped chewing. He finally realized they were not in the meadow. "Harwinton, where are we?" he asked.

"I don't know, but we'd better get out of here. There're too many humans and that usually means trouble."

They followed the walkway in the park, hoping it

would lead them out of the noise and confusion of the city. But the path ended at the side of one of those buildings with the big windows. As Harwinton poked his head around the corner to see if it was safe, Bumper glanced up at the window. To his surprise he saw animals: Puppies, cats and —

"Rabbits! Harwinton, I see rabbits!" he whispered excitedly, pointing at the building. "Come on, we have to go inside. Maybe they're my cousins."

Before the bear could stop him, Bumper was heading for the door. The cub had no choice but to follow. On the right side of the room were cages filled with hamsters, mice and guinea pigs. Next to them were tall glass tanks. Fish! Distracted, Harwinton stopped to watch them dart here and there in their watery homes. He tried to imitate their funny mouth movements. Looking at the fish reminded the cub of how hungry he was. Pushing the thought aside, he continued to look for his friend. Where was that rabbit?

In a cage in the middle of the store, sat a large green parrot that squawked and whistled as it rocked back and forth on its perch. Farther down, a small flock of parakeets chirped and flitted around excitedly when they saw the cub pass by. There was still no sign of Bumper.

His frustration and anxiety growing, Harwinton walked slowly up and down the narrow aisles.

Finally, he came to where the cages of puppies, kittens and rabbits were located. At the end of the row, he could see Bumper. Carefully, the cub squeezed past a display rack of squeaky toys. As he did so, he bumped into the side of a long, high table.

"May I help you, young man?" asked an elderly salesclerk with thick glasses on her nose. As she peered down at the 'young man', she adjusted her glasses so she could see him better. "EEK!" she screamed. "Help! There's a wild animal in the store!"

A wild animal in the store? Where? Equally frightened, Harwinton spun around. His sudden movement caused the cub's full weight to hit against the rack of squeaky toys. CRASH! Down went the rack and the toys scattered everywhere. Their high-pitched squeals of protest added to the noisy confusion as Harwinton ran over them on his way to the door.

"Call the police! Call the army!" cried the frantic salesclerk, while pressing the emergency alert button under the counter.

Commotion spread throughout the store. The puppies started barking and whining and were joined by the kittens' mewing and crying. A customer noticed a rabbit in the aisle near the rabbit cages. Thinking one of the store animals had gotten loose, the man tried to grab for the now-terrified

Bumper. Moving swiftly, the young rabbit narrowly escaped being caught as he darted out the door after his friend.

Outside, Harwinton and Bumper raced across the busy street. Motorists jammed on their brakes and honked their horns. A policeman, who knew about the escaped bear and rabbit, frantically flagged down another policeman driving by in his squad car.

"Quick! Radio for back-up," he shouted. "Those wild animals are loose in the streets."

Harwinton and Bumper continued to run as fast as their legs could carry them. Instead of the tall buildings and noisy streets of the city, trees and bushes now surrounded them. Gone were the humans with their dangerous cars and trucks. But just when they thought they were free from danger, a high-pitched squeal suddenly broke the silence.

"There they are by the side of the road," said the policeman driving the squad car.

"Turn off the siren or we'll lose them again," advised his partner.

But it was too late. Harwinton and Bumper had already disappeared into the heavily wooded area.

"Where could they have gone?" cried the driver in frustration. "They were here a minute ago."

"We'll never find them in all those trees," answered the second policeman. "It's getting too dark anyway. We'll have to call off the search until tomorrow. I'll radio in."

Harwinton and Bumper stayed very still until they knew the policemen were gone. Safe for the time being, they fell into a deep sleep.

It was now nine o'clock at night at the Stevenson home. Ranger George and Betty sat with their friends talking about the day's events.

"I wonder if the police have found those animals yet," signed Betty.

Just then, the phone rang. "I'll get it," said Johnny. A moment later, he was back in the living room. "Excuse me. It's for you, Dad. A Sergeant Brown wants to talk to you."

Explaining quickly to George and Betty, Dr. Stevenson went to the phone. "Hello, Sergeant. This is Dr. Stevenson."

"I'm sorry to bother you at this time of night, Doc, but I thought you should know what the status is." The policeman then proceeded to tell Dr. Stevenson what had happened at the pet store and the unsuccessful chase afterward. While very concerned, the doctor found himself stifling the urge to laugh. He could picture the almost comedic chaos those two animals had caused.

"Where were they last seen?" asked the doctor.

"On Woodhaven Road," answered Sergeant Brown. "Two of my men saw the cub and the rabbit before they entered the treed area. We're planning to send out a search party tomorrow; but to be honest, I don't think we're going to be successful. The woods get pretty thick out that way and it'll be tough to get through."

"Yes, I'm aware of that," said Dr. Stevenson. "How long will you search for them?"

"Maybe a day or two. If we do get any leads, of course we'll keep looking. But don't get your hopes up. As those animals keep moving, it'll get impossible to track them."

"I understand," said the doctor. "I appreciate your efforts. If my family and I can be of any help, please don't hesitate to call us."

"Thanks," answered the Sergeant. "I'll need to contact Ranger Goodwill. We sure could use his experience as well."

"He's here with his wife. I can give him the message."

"Great! That's right, you know that Sign Language stuff. I need to learn that myself. Okay. Here's what we need Ranger Goodwill to do." Dr. Stevenson wrote down the policeman's instructions and after a few more moments of conversation the two men said good night.

Returning to the living room, the doctor relayed the message to George and then told the group what the policeman had said concerning the search for the animals.

"John, we need to seek the Lord," signed Mrs. Stevenson. "While we should try to find the animals, they're really in God's hands now."

Dr. Stevenson nodded in agreement and led the group in prayer. They asked for wisdom and protection for the search party. Johnny prayed for the safety of the cub and rabbit, while Susie asked that God would lead the animals to a good home.

Afterward, to ease the somberness of the situation, they sang a song of praise to the Lord. At the end, Dr. Stevenson started to laugh uncontrollably.

"What's so funny, Daddy?" asked Susie.

Still shaking with laughter, the doctor managed to speak and sign as he told them about the animals' visit to the pet store and the chase that had followed. By the end of the story, everyone was laughing heartily and shaking their heads in disbelief.

"While I'm glad the animals made it safely to the woods," signed George, stopping to wipe tears from his eyes. "I wish I could've seen that."

"Me, too," signed Betty. "George, it's getting late. If you and John are going to join the search effort tomorrow, we'd better go home."

"You're right, dear."

"Thanks for your help, you two," said Dr. Stevenson. "Sorry things went the way they did."

"That's all right," signed George. "See you in the morning."

CHAPTER 11

The Search

Very early the next morning, the bright light of the sun awakened Harwinton. In the distance he could hear the sound of human voices and the occasional barking of a dog. Realizing they were searching for him and Bumper, Harwinton became alarmed.

"Bumper," he whispered. "Get up! They're coming for us. We have to find a better place to hide."

In an instant, the rabbit was awake and on his feet. "Harwinton, what'll we do?"

Remembering Mrs. Stevenson's words about asking for wisdom, the cub prayed a simple prayer. "God, Bumper and I are lost. Please help us and show us the way to go. Amen."

"Do you really think God will answer us?"

"Yes, I do."

"Well, I hope he doesn't take too long. Those people are getting closer." No sooner had Bumper spoken, when a bright shaft of light shone through the trees.

"The sunbeam!" they cried. They had not seen it since they had arrived at The City of Light.

"Don't you see, Bumper?" said the cub happily. "God is answering our prayer. Come on, let's follow it."

For once, Bumper didn't argue. Eagerly the two friends followed the dazzling light. From the road, the trees had looked so close together, it had seemed impossible to walk through. Now, Harwinton and Bumper were amazed at how easy the path was. As they entered a dense section of bushes, they both realized the sound of the human voices and the barking dog was growing fainter and fainter.

"Looks like they were here, Doc," said Sergeant Brown, stopping at the tree under which the cub and rabbit had slept. "There's some tufts of hair from the cub's fur and the leaves on the ground show two indentations."

"Officer Jones' dog is picking up a scent," noticed Dr. Stevenson. "Let's see what direction it takes."

The K-9 Officer let his dog sniff at the ground for a few more minutes until it was ready to move on.

Then barking excitedly, the dog began to walk down the same trail Harwinton and Bumper had taken earlier that morning. Sergeant Brown and Dr. Stevenson followed close behind, keeping their eyes open for more clues. When they came to a dense thicket of bushes, the dog stopped. Appearing confused, it couldn't decide whether to continue on ahead or go in another direction. A few moments later, Ranger Goodwill and two other police officers met up with Dr. Stevenson's group.

"What's going on with the dog?" asked Sergeant Brown.

"I'm not really sure," answered the K-9 Officer. "It seems he's picking up other animal scents now."

"The wind is blowing stronger since we've started," commented Dr. Stevenson. "That could be what's causing the problem."

Ranger Goodwill stood quietly by, lip-reading the men's conversation. As he watched, a gentle prodding stirred deep within him and he closed his eyes briefly in prayer. Nodding in agreement with the Still Small Voice he could hear in his heart, he opened his eyes. Motioning to get Dr. Stevenson's attention, he signed that he needed to speak to the officers.

"Excuse me, Sergeant Brown," said Dr. Stevenson. "George has something to tell us."

"By all means," responded the Sergeant. "He's an expert when it comes to these woods."

"Will you voice for me, John?" asked George.

The doctor nodded and gestured for him to continue. "While you were talking," spoke Dr. Stevenson as Ranger Goodwill signed, "I asked God what to do. From this point, if we go any farther we are in danger of getting into some hidden swampland. The animals will probably make it through safely, but I strongly suggest that we stop the search and turn back. We will have to let God take care of what he created."

The policemen were silent for a few minutes. Sergeant Brown was the first to speak. "I trust Ranger Goodwill's judgment," he said. "And I agree. We need to let God take care of those animals now. Gentlemen, our work here is done."

The men turned and started back down the trail toward their vehicles. The K-9 officer patted his dog. "You tried, boy. It's okay. Good job."

Sergeant Brown found himself next to Dr. Stevenson. "I really would like to know Sign Language," he said. "How long did it take you to learn?"

"About a year. You have to work at it, but it's worth it. I'm glad I know people like George and Betty Goodwill. They have such a strong faith and trust in God. They've been good examples for me and my family."

"Would you have time to teach me to sign?"

"Sure. Just let me know when you want to get started."

When they reached the road, the policemen said good-bye to Ranger Goodwill and Dr. Stevenson and thanked them for their help. On the drive home in the doctor's station wagon, George noticed his friend was extra quiet and his expression appeared sad.

"What's wrong, John?" he asked.

"George, I don't know why, but I feel like I failed those two animals. We came so close to getting them to a safe, new home at The Lighted Forest. Why couldn't it have worked out that we would find them this morning?"

"I understand how you feel, but remember God's ways are not our ways. He knows what's best for all his creation."

"You signed that as if you know something," said John. Glancing at George, he noticed the ranger had a broad grin on his face. "Okay, what's up?"

"You know those bushes we stopped at?"

"Yeah. What about them?"

"They lead to somewhere."

"Yes, to the swampland."

"True, but what's beyond the swampland? Understand?"

Dr. Stevenson thought for a moment, then it hit him what George was talking about. "Praise the

Lord!" John shouted joyfully as he turned down the street to his home. "God is good!"

"All the time," signed George as he joined John in hearty laughter.

When John pulled into the driveway, Mrs. Stevenson, the children and Betty were waiting for them in the front yard.

"Did you find the animals, Dad?" asked Johnny hopefully.

"No, son, we didn't. We tried, but it would've been too dangerous to continue, so we decided to stop."

Johnny looked thoughtful for a moment. "You know, Dad, somehow I think they *are* going to be all right."

"Yes, they will be," answered Dr. Stevenson as he hugged his son.

"You both must be hungry and tired," said Mrs. Stevenson. "Betty and I made ham and cheese sandwiches and there's hot coffee ready on the stove."

Before they sat down at the dining room table, Dr. Stevenson asked George to say grace. "Thank you, Lord, for this day and the food you've provided. Bless it and the hands that prepared it. Thank you also, Lord, for a way through the swampland to a place of safety and rest. In Jesus' name. Amen."

"Amen," said everyone.

Later, before going to bed, Susie climbed onto

her Daddy's lap to give him a good-night hug and kiss. "Daddy, when Ranger George prayed at lunch today about the Lord making a way through the swampland, did it have something to do with the animals?"

Dr. Stevenson smiled. "Yes, honey, it did."

"You know what I think Ranger George meant, Daddy," said Susie. "I think he meant that God has a home for them and he'll make sure they get there."

"You surely are a smart little girl." The clock on the wall softly chimed ten times. "It's getting late, Susie. Run along to bed now."

"Okay, Daddy. Good night. I love you."

"Good night, Susie. I love you, too."

At the doorway to the living room, Susie turned around. "Will we ever see the little bear and rabbit again?"

"Maybe. You never know what God will do. Sweet dreams, honey."

Dr. Stevenson sat for a long time thinking about the day. While he still wished he had been successful in helping the animals, he realized now that God had a purpose in having things happen the way they did. What that purpose was to accomplish, God would reveal in his time and in his way. But one thing was certain; He would make a way through the swampland. Yes, thought Dr. Stevenson with a smile, God *is* good.

CHAPTER 12

The Lighted Forest

Staying close together and keeping their eyes on the sunbeam, Harwinton and Bumper made it safely through the swampland. They had been walking for some time now, when they heard the babbling of a brook. Thirsty and tired, they took a long drink of the cool water and lay down on the grass for a much-needed rest. A gentle breeze had begun to blow bringing a new and different sound.

"Did you hear something?" asked Bumper, sitting up to listen.

Before Harwinton could answer, a jolly singing voice came echoing from upstream. The voice belonged to a beaver that was swimming in the water:

"Osborne A. Gain! Yes, that is my name!
Osborne A. Gain! I'll never be the same.
Since Jesus came and took my sins away—
Osborne A. Gain! And it's a brand new
day!"

With all his might, the beaver started the song again. He didn't realize he had an audience until he happened to look up at the end of the third time. "Hello!" he called, a big grin on his face. "I'm Osborne A. Gain. What can I do for you?"

Harwinton and Bumper introduced themselves. On the bank, near where Osborne had been swimming, they noticed some freshly caught fish. Food! They hadn't eaten much the last few days and it sure looked good.

"Have you young fellers had lunch yet?" asked Osborne, picking up the fish he had caught.

"No, we haven't," answered Harwinton.

"Then come with me."

They followed Osborne to a blue-and-white cloth spread out on the grass under a pine tree. On the cloth were carrots and honey, more fish and freshly picked clover. The beaver said a short prayer of thanks and invited the bear and rabbit to help themselves. As they ate, two other animals, a pair of otters, walked by. They greeted Osborne and waved to Harwinton and Bumper.

"Allow me to introduce my friends to you," said Osborne to his guests. He motioned to the animals to come over. "This is Ann Otter Christian and her husband, Andrew."

"How do you do?" asked Ann. "Welcome to The Lighted Forest."

Harwinton and Bumper stared at each other in shocked surprise. Sensing their concern, Andrew assured them, "Yes, this is The Lighted Forest. What brings you here? Can we be of any help?"

"You don't know anything about us," snapped the rabbit. "What makes you think we need help?"

"Bumper," answered Osborne calmly, "all of us need help with something. And from the looks of you and Harwinton, the two of you have been through a pretty rough time. Why don't you tell us about it?"

Osborne and the otters were so friendly, that the bear and rabbit found themselves telling their whole story from the beginning. To Harwinton's and Bumper's surprise the others knew of Dr. Stevenson and Tobiah T. Owl.

"Tobiah teaches us about the Bible every Sunday," explained Ann. "He lives here in The Lighted Forest."

"And Dr. Stevenson's a wonderful human," remarked Andrew. "He's one of the doctors for the animals here. He took care of Ann when she hurt her leg last spring."

"Yes," agreed Ann. "He tries very hard to do the right thing. There's another special human who works here at the forest. His name is Ranger Goodwill. He can't hear, so he talks with his hands. He's so kind to all of us."

"Is he a tall, gray-haired man?" asked Harwinton.

"That's him," said Osborne. "He and Dr. Stevenson are friends. Seems like the two of you were in good hands. Why did you run away from them? They wouldn't have hurt you. Both of them are good Christian men."

"How were we to know that?" retorted Bumper. "What is this Christian thing all about anyway? At the Stevenson's house they were always praying. They would thank God for this and praise the Lord for that. I thought they really wanted to help us find our families, until they said they were going to..." Bumper stopped as he realized that he and Harwinton had arrived at the very place Dr. Stevenson had wanted to take them.

Osborne quietly finished his sentence for him, "bring you here to The Lighted Forest." Feeling very foolish, the rabbit nodded.

"But isn't it wonderful," exclaimed Ann, "how God got you here in spite of your running away! God is awesome!"

"Osborne, who is Jesus?" asked Harwinton. "The

Stevensons talked a lot about him and we heard his name in your song this morning. Who is he?"

"Jesus is God's son," answered Ann.

"God has a son?" asked Bumper, a puzzled look on his face.

"Yes," said Andrew. "Haven't the two of you ever learned anything about God and the Bible?"

"No," answered Harwinton, feeling a little embarrassed. "Living in The Dark Forest we didn't think much about God, let alone have someone to teach us. One time, when I was a little cub, my Poppa told me how God had created the whole world. But after that, Poppa never mentioned God again."

"How sad!" exclaimed Ann. "But there's no reason why we couldn't tell you about Jesus right now."

"Amen!" agreed Osborne. "Your Poppa was right, Harwinton. God did create the whole world. Have you ever heard of Adam and Eve?"

"No," answered the cub.

"Well," continued Osborne, "they were the first humans God created after the animals. Adam and Eve lived in a beautiful place called The Garden of Eden. God told them they could eat of every tree in the garden except for *one* certain tree. He warned them if they ate from that tree they would surely die."

"Was the fruit on it bad?" asked Bumper.

"No," answered the beaver, "but God knew it

wouldn't be good for them."

"Then, one day," added Andrew, continuing the lesson, "the devil, who is God's enemy, used a snake in the garden to lie to Eve. He said she and Adam wouldn't die if they ate from the tree, but they would become like God. Eve listened to the snake and went to the tree. She took some fruit and ate it. Then she gave some to Adam and he ate."

"You mean they disobeyed God, like I disobey my Momma and Poppa sometimes?" asked Harwinton.

"Yes," answered Andrew. "However, this was much more serious. Their disobedience brought a bad thing called sin into the world and caused a separation between God and his creation."

"Being separated feels awful," said Bumper, thinking of his family.

"It sure does," agreed Harwinton. "But how does Jesus fit into all this?"

"You see," explained Ann, "God loved the world so much, he decided to send His only Son, named Jesus, to heal the separation. Jesus was willing to suffer and die on a cross to take the sin away. Because of what he did, there is now a way back to God by accepting and believing in his Son."

"When we do that," added Osborne, "we become what the Bible calls 'born again' and are adopted into God's family."

"Oh!" exclaimed Harwinton. "So that's why your name is Osborne A. Gain."

"Yes," said the beaver, chuckling. "I want others to know I believe in Jesus."

"So what does Christian mean?" asked Bumper.

"Jesus has many names," explained Osborne. "One of them is The Christ. Those who follow Jesus are called Christians."

"Then that explains Ann's name," said Harwinton, with a smile. "Because she's an *other* Christian."

"Exactly," answered Ann. The otter began to sing the same tune Osborne had sung earlier, only this time she changed the words:

> *"Be born again and God will change your name.*
> *Be born again—you'll never be the same.*
> *Let Jesus come and take your sins from you,*
> *Then you will be Ann Otter Christian, too!"*

Harwinton, Osborne and the Otters laughed heartily, while Bumper could only manage an uncertain smile.

"I want to accept Jesus," decided Harwinton. "Would you tell me how?"

"It's simple," answered Andrew. "Ask Jesus to

forgive you for all the bad things you've done. Then ask him to come into your heart."

The cub bowed his head and closing his eyes, prayed to ask Jesus into his heart. After he was finished, he had a worried look on his face.

"What's wrong?" asked Osborne.

"I'm so angry at the campers who started the fire. It's their fault Bumper and I lost our homes. How do I stop being mad at them?"

"When I'm angry with someone," said Ann, "I choose to forgive them."

"But it's hard..."

"Sometimes it is hard to forgive others when they've hurt us; but Jesus' love is so great that he forgave us even when he was on the cross. If we follow Jesus, he expects us to forgive as he did. Ask him to help you, Harwinton."

Taking a deep breath, the young bear started slowly. "Jesus, please help me to stop being angry at the campers. I choose to forgive them because you forgave me. Amen."

"Do you feel better now?" asked Andrew.

To Harwinton's surprise he felt lighter inside. "Yeah!" he cried. "I'm not mad at them anymore. Thank you, Jesus." Happily, the bear began to sing:

"I'm born again; God has changed my name.

I'm born again; I'll never be the same.
Since Jesus came and took my sins away,
I'm born again and it's a brand new day!"

Delighted, Ann and Andrew clapped while Osborne danced around as Harwinton sang it again.

"My friend," said the beaver excitedly, "today you do have a new name. Everyone, meet Harwinton *Christian* Bear."

As Bumper watched the others joyfully celebrating, he tried to understand. He wanted to pray, too, but he just couldn't.

"What's the matter?" asked Osborne, going over to the rabbit.

"I want to believe, but I don't see how God could see us through everything and still have taken our families away."

"Don't say that," said Harwinton. "They could still be alive somewhere. God took care of us; he had to have taken care of them, too."

"Be we *haven't* found them," persisted Bumper, starting to cry. "Then we heard Dr. Stevenson say that The Dark Forest rangers gave up looking for the bears and rabbits a long time ago. We needed a home and were on our way back to The Shaded Forest when we ended up here."

"You mustn't give up," encouraged Ann. "And we hope you'll stay with us."

"The bear and rabbit families here are really nice," added Andrew. "We could take you and Harwinton to meet them. I'm sure they'd have room for one more."

"No, thanks," sniffed the rabbit tearfully. "It just wouldn't be the same."

"Let's ask God to help him," whispered Osborne.

Harwinton joined the beaver and the otters and the four of them prayed for Bumper. The poor rabbit sobbed and sobbed. Ann put her arm around him.

"It's all right, Bumper," she said softly. "God knows you're confused and scared. Someday soon, I believe you'll be ready to accept Jesus. When you do, he'll be there waiting to welcome you."

"What if I'm never ready?"

"Just wait and see," answered Andrew. "God knows what to do."

The afternoon had passed quickly. Osborne invited Harwinton and Bumper to come and stay with him for awhile.

"We don't want to put you in danger," said Harwinton. "There were policemen with a dog looking for us, remember?"

"I happen to know they've called off the search," said the beaver.

"What?" exclaimed Harwinton and Bumper.

"Yes. Tobiah saw the search party leave. As soon as he knew they were really gone, he stopped by my place and told me to be on the lookout for two runaway animals—a bear and a rabbit. That's why I was near the stream this afternoon. I knew who you were as soon as I saw you."

"But how did you know *where* to find us?" asked Bumper. Osborne gave him a wide grin. "Oh," said the rabbit, realizing the answer to his own question, "Jesus told you."

"Who else?" answered Osborne, laughing. "He knows everything and sees everything. I sure am glad he told me where to look, because I'm really happy to know you boys. Come on, time for some shut-eye."

For the first time in many days, peace surrounded the bear and rabbit. But Bumper couldn't sleep.

"I don't know, Harwinton," he said anxiously. "This all seems nice, but I just don't understand."

"Don't give up, Bumper. Give it a little time."

"Okay. I will."

A few days passed. The cub loved The Lighted Forest and began to feel at home. He looked forward to Osborne taking him to meet the Bear family on Sunday. The rabbit, however, continued to struggle with his doubts and fears.

One night, before they went to sleep, Bumper said, "Harwinton, I'm glad that you like it here. But I just don't seem to fit in. I've decided to try to find my way back to The Shaded Forest."

"Bumper, don't," pleaded Harwinton. "Wait until you've met the other rabbits and then see how you feel."

"I'm sorry. My mind is made up. I'm leaving tomorrow."

"You can't go alone. I'll go, too."

"No," insisted the rabbit. "You wouldn't be happy at the other place. You stay. I have to do what's best for me."

Harwinton realized it was useless to try to convince his friend to change his plans. He lay awake for a long time praying to God to help Bumper believe.

CHAPTER 13

A Miracle for Bumper

Very early the next morning, Bumper got up and quietly left Osborne's home. The sun was just beginning to rise. Since there was only one path, Bumper started down it. Harwinton, who had only pretended to still be asleep, was following his friend at a safe distance.

Bumper had walked for a short time, when the path suddenly forked. "Now which way do I go?" he wondered aloud. "Right or left?"

"Pardon me," called a voice. "Could I be of any assistance?" Bumper looked up as a huge bird swooped down to him from a tall oak tree.

"M-Mr. Owl!" exclaimed the rabbit. "What are

you doing here?"

"I live in this part of the forest," answered Tobiah. "It's good to see you again, Bumper. Where's your friend Harwinton?"

"Back there with Osborne. Harwinton's staying, but I'm going."

While Bumper was speaking, Tobiah spotted the cub hiding behind a clump of bushes. Harwinton shook his head and motioned to the owl not to let on that he was there. Understanding, Tobiah nodded to him. Looking at Bumper, the owl said sadly, "I'm sorry to hear that you're going away, my little friend."

"I don't fit in here," explained the rabbit, trying not to cry. "I want to be a Christian, too, but I don't understand how God can be good, if my family is gone."

"There are many things about God we don't understand," replied the owl, "but that doesn't mean he isn't good to us. Have you tried looking for your families here in The Lighted Forest?"

"No, but what if they're not here? I don't want to get my hopes up, only to be disappointed again."

"I can understand that," said Tobiah. "But if you don't at least try to look for them before you leave, you'll always wonder."

"I suppose that's true," admitted Bumper. He thought about it for a few moments. "No. I'm too tired to look anymore. I don't know why God led us all the way here for noth..."

"BUMPER! IS THAT YOU?" screamed an excited voice from the path to the right. "Momma! Poppa! It's Bumper!"

Before Bumper could realize what was happening, his youngest sister, Bunni, was hugging her long-lost brother and dancing him around for joy. Then Bumper felt himself being picked up by familiar, loving arms that squeezed him tight. A stunned Harwinton watched from his hiding place behind the bushes.

"We've been praying so hard to find you," cried Momma Rabbit. "Thank you, God, for answering us."

Bumper, who at first had been too surprised to speak, was laughing and crying at the same time. "Wait!" he exclaimed. "I've got to go get Harwinton."

"Harwinton?" asked Poppa Rabbit in amazement. "He's here, too?"

"Yes. We've been together since the fire."

Tobiah called to the lone figure, hiding behind the bushes. "You can come out now."

The Rabbit family ran to hug their son's friend. "Harwinton," sobbed Mrs. Rabbit. "Thank God, you're all right. Your family has been so worried."

"My family?" asked the cub. "You mean they're here at The Lighted Forest?"

"Yes, dear," answered Mrs. Rabbit. "We live next to them in our new homes. Come, we'll take you to them."

Tobiah flew overhead, hooting for joy. A robin picked up the message and started singing. Swooping and flitting around the forest, she happily spread the word, "God has done a miracle. At last, Harwinton and Bumper are reunited with their families." Osborne and the Otters shouted praises and high-fived each other when they heard it.

"Way to go, God!" whistled Osborne.

The scene at the Bear family's den was the same as at the path: hugs, tears, kisses and more thanks to the Lord. After everyone had quieted down, Harwinton and Bumper told their families about their long journey.

Holding Harwinton close again, Momma Bear said tearfully, "We thought you were lost."

"We knew where we were all the time, Momma, but we couldn't find *you*."

"How did you get here?" asked Bumper.

"After the fire," explained Poppa Bear, "we went back to try to find Harwinton. We looked everywhere."

"We had gone back also to search for you, Bumper," added Poppa Rabbit, "when we happened upon Harwinton's family near the old den."

"That's right," said Poppa Bear. "All of us had just about given up, when this old owl called to us..."

"Tobiah!" exclaimed Harwinton and Bumper.

The owl blushed with embarrassment. "I didn't do anything special," he murmured.

"Yes," continued Poppa Bear. "It was Tobiah. He was perched up in that giant tree behind the den. You remember that tree, don't you, son? Tobiah asked us who we were looking for."

"We sadly told him about you and Bumper," said Momma Bear, picking up the story. "To our surprise, Tobiah said he had spoken to you that very morning. He showed us the trail you had taken and told us to come here, to The Lighted Forest, where we would find you."

"But if you were following the same trail as we were, why didn't we meet?" asked Harwinton.

"Yeah!" agreed Bumper. "Did you see a fox and a place called The Shaded Forest?"

"No," answered Poppa Bear in a soft voice. "You see, before Harwinton was born, we used to live here with Grandma and Grandpa Bear. Then I chose to move away to The Dark Forest. I once knew the trail that would by-pass Pretender and The Shaded Forest. Tobiah showed me the way again."

"Poppa," said Harwinton, "Bumper and I found your pocket-watch, but then we lost it."

"That's all right, son," replied Poppa Bear. "The most important thing is that we've not only found each other, but we've also found our way back to

God."

"Because of what Jesus did," said Harwinton.

"Yes, son," answered Poppa Bear, wiping away a tear.

After a few more hugs and kisses, Bumper wiggled out of his mother's tight grasp and hurried over to Tobiah. "Mr. Owl," said the rabbit, "I'm sorry I doubted. Can I be a Christian, too? Is there room for me?"

"Bumper, there's room for anyone who wants to follow Jesus."

"Then may I become one now, please?"

"Of course."

Everyone joined paws while Tobiah prayed with the young rabbit. "You know," continued the owl, when they had finished praying, "your Poppa told me you have lots of names, and that Bumper is only your nickname."

"Yeah," answered the rabbit dejectedly. "But I don't like my real one."

"Did you know that each one of your names has its own special meaning?"

"They do?"

"Yes. Would you like me to show you what they are?"

"Okay."

Tobiah took out his Bible and opened it to a section that gave the definitions of names, places and other words used in the Scriptures. "Now, let's see," began the owl. "Your first name is Benjamin. It means 'son of the right hand.' When you left The Dark Forest, you told us you took the path to your right."

Bumper nodded.

"Your second name is Uriah. This one means 'God is light.' Wasn't there a bright sunbeam that led you and Harwinton on your travels?"

"Yeah! There was!" exclaimed the rabbit, his interest starting to grow. "What about my third name, Mr. Owl?"

"Maaziah means 'God is a refuge.' Didn't you find shelter from the fierce storm in the large pile of rocks at the edge of the meadow?"

"We did!" cried Bumper. "What's Peh—uh, Peka—I can't pronounce it."

"Pek-a-hi-ah," said Tobiah slowly. "Its meaning is 'God has opened the eyes.' God *has* opened your eyes, Bumper, to the truth of his everlasting love for us."

"And Elisha?" asked the rabbit eagerly.

"Elisha means 'God is salvation,' which He has provided for us through His Son, Jesus."

"WOW!" shouted Bumper, dancing up and down for joy. "I *like* my real name!"

"Aren't you glad now that we didn't go back to The Shaded Forest?" asked Harwinton.

"I sure am," answered the rabbit, hugging his friend. "God is good!"

CHAPTER 14

Home At Last

Two days after the search had been called off, Dr. Stevenson stopped by to see Ranger Goodwill at The Lighted Forest.

"Hi, John," signed George. "Good to see you."

"I was on my way home and thought I'd stop by. Any news about the cub and the rabbit?"

"No, not yet. But I will call you if they show up, I promise."

"I don't mean to bother you, but I'm worried about them."

"It's all right, John. No problem. I understand. I'll take a ride out on Sunday and do some investigating."

"Thanks. I'd better go now. See you later."

"Later," signed George. "Take care of yourself."

Early Sunday afternoon, the sky was overcast and threatened to storm at any moment. True to his word, Ranger George took a ride to the clearing. He parked the jeep and got out. Slowly, he walked around, stopping now and then to peer through the binoculars that hung around his neck. As he adjusted the lenses to get a better view of some pine trees, a sudden movement got his attention. In the distance, he could see a family of bears moving down the path in front of the pine trees. Bringing the binoculars back up to his face, he zeroed in on the bears.

There should be six of them, thought George. He counted as they passed by. One, two, three, four, five, six, seven. Seven? Walking beside the last bear was a young, cottontail rabbit. "Praise the Lord!" voiced George. "Thank you, Jesus!"

Laughing for joy, the Ranger returned to his jeep and hurried back to the station. Sitting down at the desk, he dialed Dr. Stevenson's number. Anxiously he waited for the red light on the teletypewriter (TTY) machine to glow steadily. Ah! Finally! He tapped the space bar several times to signal John to use his TTY.

"hello ga" Came the slowly typed message.

"HELLO THIS IS RANGER GOODWILL IS JOHN THERE Q GA"

"hi george this is john what's up q ga"

"COULD YOU AND YOUR FAMILY COME

RIGHT AWAY Q GA"

"is anything wrong q ga"

"I WILL SHOW YOU WHEN YOU GET HERE GA"

Knowing George would not call him unless it was very important, John typed back they would come as soon as possible.

"GOOD. WILL BE WAITING BYE SK."

"bye sksk."

The doctor ripped the paper from the TTY printer and reread the brief conversation. What did George need to show them? Dr. Stevenson hurried to the stairs that led to the children's bedrooms. "Johnny!" he called. "Get your sisters and meet us out near the driveway. Now, please."

"Coming, Dad!"

"What is it, John?" asked Mrs. Stevenson, who had just finished the dinner dishes.

"George just called. He wants us to come out to the ranger station right away."

"Did he say why?"

"No, only that he'd show us when we got there."

"I'll get my coat."

On the way to The Lighted Forest, Johnny, Susie and Joy made a game out of trying to guess the mystery. Susie thought it had something to do with the bear and rabbit.

"We'll find out soon enough," said Dr. Stevenson,

his hopes beginning to rise.

As he parked the station wagon next to Ranger Goodwill's jeep, rain began to pour down heavily. George and Betty appeared on the porch and helped the Stevensons get inside. Suddenly, a huge bolt of lightning split the sky causing the lights to go out. Joy hid her face in her mother's coat.

"It's all right, honey," soothed Mrs. Stevenson. "We're safe."

"It should be over soon," signed Betty as George lit a lantern so they could see. "The weather report said the storm was a fast moving one."

"Then we'll take a drive out to the clearing," said George, trying not to smile.

A few minutes later, the rain slowed to a drizzle and the thunder began to die down. To Joy's relief, the lights came back on. "Yay!" she cried as she looked up from her hiding place.

"Let's go," signed George.

Ranger Goodwill and Dr. Stevenson got into the jeep while Mrs. Stevenson, Betty and the children followed in the station wagon. The drive to the clearing was short. Parking the two vehicles near each other, they all got out and started walking up a little hill. From the hill, they had a better view of the trees. Straight ahead, Mrs. Stevenson caught sight of a group of animals.

"John!" she whispered excitedly. "Over there!"

Dr. Stevenson's gaze followed to where his wife was pointing. Under the pine trees, he could make out a family of bears and rabbits sitting together. Taking the binoculars from around his neck, George handed them to his friend.

"Look," signed George, a big grin on his face.

Dr. Stevenson focused in on the animals. In the middle of the group he saw a young cub and rabbit. "It's them!" he said, holding back the urge to shout. "Can we try to get closer?"

George nodded. "But it's best just you and I go," he signed. "Too many people may scare them away."

Walking slowly to avoid startling the animals, the two men started down the hill. They stopped at a large pile of rocks and hid behind them. From there, Dr. Stevenson was able to clearly see the two animals that had been in his home.

"Thank you, Lord," he signed, greatly relieved to know they had made it safely through the swampland.

"Amen," answered George.

Harwinton had noticed the humans approaching. He recognized the doctor who had tried to help them.

"Bumper," he whispered. "Isn't that Dr. Stevenson?"

"Where?"

"There. Near the rocks. Ranger Goodwill's with him."

Bumper nodded, a thoughtful look on his face. Osborne's words about Dr. Stevenson being a good Christian man came back to him. "Harwinton, we need to let him know we're sorry we ran away."

The cub agreed. "Come on."

"Where are you boys going?" asked Poppa Bear.

"To make peace with someone," answered Harwinton. "We'll be right back."

"John," signed George excitedly, "they're coming to us."

The two men quietly came out from behind the rocks and stood very still. Harwinton and Bumper stopped a few feet away. Moving slowly, Dr. Stevenson approached them and stooped down. Then very gently, the bear and rabbit nuzzled against his outstretched hands. Tears filled the doctor's eyes. "Praise God," he whispered as he stroked their soft fur.

At that moment, the sun came out. In the eastern sky there appeared a beautiful rainbow. From the top of the hill, Johnny and Susie cheered with delight. Joining hands with little Joy, they began to dance around on the grass, singing the song the bear and rabbit had heard that day in the meadow.

Sing Alleluia! Praise to the Lord! Harwinton and Bumper had found a home—now and forevermore.

Amen.

A Message from Harwinton

Dear Friends,

Thank you for letting Bumper and me share our adventures with you. All of us here at The Lighted Forest want you to know that God loves you and that you, too, can become born again into his family by asking Jesus into your heart. Please share this story with someone you know who is separated from God. Let them know "There is room for anyone who wants to follow Jesus."

Love,

Harwinton

Printed in the United States
22360LVS00001BD/184-225